CONSTELLATION ROSE

A NOVEL

SHARON M. CLARKE

Clarke Books
Anna Maria Island, Florida

Cover design, interior design, and eBook
by Blue Harvest Creative
www.blueharvestcreative.com

Edited by Clarke Books

CONSTELLATION ROSE

Published by
Clarke Books

ISBN-13: 978-1500431235
ISBN-10: 1500431230

Visit the author at:
www.clarkebooks.net

ALSO BY

SHARON M. CLARKE

MOURNING REDEMPTION

MORGAN'S CROSSING

COMING 2015

THE SHADOW MAN

Dedicated to my father, Homer Ping,
who passed from this life with a prayer
on his lips and without a complaint.

Everything I accomplish is dedicated to his memory.
I love you, Dad.

PROLOGUE

THE CITY OF BRIDGES, THE CITY OF HOPE

In 1917 President Theodore Roosevelt gave a poignant speech before Pittsburgh's Chamber of Commerce; "There is no more typical American city than Pittsburgh. And Pittsburgh, by its Americanism, gives a lesson to the entire United States. Pittsburgh has not been built up by talking about it. Your tremendous concerns were built by men who actually did the work. You made Pittsburgh ace high when it could have been deuce high. There is not a Pittsburgh man who did not earn his success through his deeds."

The men who comprised Pittsburgh came from all parts of the United States, Europe, Great Britain and the world. Among the Europeans and Britannia came Germans, Italians, Englishmen, Armenians, Czechs, Greeks, Irishmen, Welshmen, Hungarians, Poles, Latvians, Estonians and more. It was their sweat and blood that built Pittsburgh, making it one of the greatest industrial cities the world has ever known. Pittsburgher's toiled in the coalmines, the steel mills, the glassworks and a whole host of factories that lined the banks of the three great rivers that converged there.

The Monongahela, the Allegany, and the Ohio rivers swift currents were appreciated for the prosperity they brought despite their menacing spring floods. Unencumbered by the pollution billowing out of the various smokestacks scattered along their rivers banks, Pittsburghers endured the trials of living in and around the city with vigor and came out the other end the better man for it. Their might was only exceeded by their sheer determination and grit.

CHAPTER ONE
OUR EARLY DAYS

I was born Rose Elizabeth Evans, at three fifty-nine one rainy September afternoon in industrialized Pittsburgh, amongst its many mills and chimneys. The Great War had ended and the industrial age had begun when my parents met and fell in love after a relatively short courtship. They were wed in an informal ceremony at the city hall just after Christmas one bright and promising day in early January. Their small but festive wedding reception consisted of a few good friends, a two tiered cake, and some beer. The modest gala was held in the unassuming basement of the friend's home who also served as their witness and signed the marriage certificate. I happened onto the scene later that same year, the eldest daughter of Geraint and Dorothy Evans.

Father was the one that took credit for calling me Rose, but to everyone else I was simply Rosie. My parents teased that when I was born I was such an ugly baby that they felt compelled to name me after a symbol of beauty to counterbalance my offence to society. For father, Rose Elizabeth fit the bill. Mother insisted that she would have preferred to name me after her mother but that she was overridden by father who did not care for the name,

Gertrude Edna. Now I am quite sure that Gertrude was a beautiful woman but why strap me with a name like that. Father may not have won many arguments with mother but I was always thankful he won that one. I, like my father, could never imagine me as a Gertrude, let alone a Gertrude Edna and am very comfortable with the name Rose Elizabeth.

The story went that when I was born the doctor used forceps to aid in my delivery and had pried me out by my forehead like a dentist pulls a rotten tooth out of its socket. Mom claimed that the forceps resembled a pair of fancy ice tongs. She said they worked and did the trick in getting me out but that they sure did not do my face any good. By the time I had made my debut appearance to the waiting arms of my anxious parents my soft head had taken on an odd elongated shape that soon went back to normal but that the shock of my heads deformity and the likes curbed their enthusiasm about becoming parents right away.

By the time my father was allowed into the room to see his little bundle of joy for the very first time he could not help notice the look of befuddlement on his brides face. There mom sat looking confused while holding their newborn baby girl wrapped in swaddling cloth. Father joked that when mother peeled back the receiving blanket for my grand unveiling he instinctively jumped back and considered contacting The Barnum and Bailey Circus where they might have earned some money exhibiting me in one of their sideshows.

The use of the forceps had made my tender eyelids blow up like a pair of balloons ready to burst from the pressure and there were signs of the grotesque bruising that was yet to come. A few days after my birth my still swollen eyelids had turned a nasty shade of purplish black with just a hint of sickly yellow added to the objectionable kaleidoscope of color that was my pitiful face. According to my folks my oddly shaped head and eyes were only a part of my apparent disfigurement and as it so happened my feet were curled up to my shinbones and were in as much of a mess as my face.

It all might have been comical if only I was not their child. They teased that they had considered switching babies but that there were no newborns available in the nursery at the time. Their doctor explained to them that my feet were turned up as the result of how mom carried me and that in time they would fall back into place. Dad joked that my tiny tootsies were stuck up against my shinbones so tight they looked like a compacted accordion or a folded shirt ready to be tucked away in a drawer. Either way, neither description sounded very attractive and ironically for the first few months of my life I slept in a dresser drawer that they were using as a makeshift cradle until they could afford one second hand crib. For them the drawer was perfect when guest came by for all they had to do to conceal my existence was to push the drawer closed and shut their bedroom door. Whenever they told me these stories I always knew they were joking, or at least I was pretty sure they were. Needless to say, there were no early baby pictures of me lying around in some obscure family album and I was nearly a year old before my pitiful puss graced a photographers' lens.

Mother and father's reminiscing of my numerous birthing mishaps could have really hurt my feelings had my feet not unfolded and my eye lids remained horribly swollen and discolored. Fortunately for me, and I suppose for them too, my apparent disfigurement only lasted a month or so and I actually grew to be an attractive baby whom they were proud to show off to their friends, neighbors and passerby's. Their horror stories became part of my makeup and were in all likelihood at least partly responsible for father labeling me as "one tough nut."

My mother was born Dorothy Eloise Stillwater and was raised for most of her young life on a Cherokee Indian Reservation in Chillicothe, Missouri. Dorothy was only part Indian but she did tout the silky Raven black hair associated with the Cherokee tribe. Instead of brown eyes mothers were strikingly green and gorgeous which made her stand out amongst other women of the day. With a flawless complexion and exquisite taste mother exhibited a flirtatious confidence that could draw men around her like bees to a honey pot. A high-spirited quick tempered woman who always spoke her mind and could destroy you with the wag of her wickedly sharp tongue. She could be ferocious and as intense as a dueling master whirling his epee. Effortlessly, mother could cut your heart out with exact precision and laugh in your face as you crumbled to the ground dying. Her very nature epitomized that there is a very fine line between love and hate and anyone that crossed that line would never be forgiven or forgotten as she possessed the memory of an elephant. A person would be lucky to have her for a friend, albeit she had few but heaven help you if you ever became her enemy. Once her love soured towards you there would be no mercy for mercy's sake and as far as she was concerned, you would be dead to her. In my mom's eyes, everything was red or it was white, there was no pink or gray in her world and she regarded compromise as a weakness that she would never consider, respect or honor. Because mother's maiden name was Stillwater, father always joked that in her case still waters not only ran deep, they ran icy cold as well.

As a child mother faced great prejudice. The unfair reproach associated with the Cherokee people hardened mother's heart triggering her survival skills which protected her against the needless bias and bigotry she'd seen going on all around. Trust did not come easy for mother. Her family had been swindled and lied to far too often for her to believe in very many people. Whenever she let her guard down, which was not often, she would expose a kinder, softer side that few could appreciate. While the world as a whole may not have experienced her love, we did. She loved us and we loved her despite her austere mannerisms.

There were six brothers and five sisters that made up the Stillwater family. Their eldest was Earl, followed by my mother Dorothy and then Walter, Florence, Eleanor, Carl, Bud, Ray, Ruby, Luke and then finally the last of the Stillwater brood was Brenda. Their mother, Gertrude Edna Stillwater died a few hours after Brenda was born. Her husband Jessup was at her side when she passed and fell into a deep mourning. The untimely death of his beloved wife caused Jessup to take to the bottle and without regard for his living children, drank himself into a coma from which he never regained consciousness. Jessup died and was buried with his wife and their two sons, Walter and Luke who had preceded them in death.

During the winter blast of 1901 the youngest member of the Stillwater family, Brenda, caught pneumonia and died. That first year after losing their parents the older siblings had miscalculated how much wood they would need to fuel the house and ran out of timber just as the worst of the three day blizzard hit. It was late January when the ice storm started. The gusty frigid winds and ice prevented them from venturing out in search of more firewood and so as a substitute they began busting up the furniture and burned it. When that fuel ran out the temperature inside the cabin plummeted and young Brenda fell ill. The nine siblings hunkered down trying their best to keep warm till the morning but their best was not good enough for Brenda who had developed a chesty cough and a high fever. Rather than removing the blankets to cool her body down they panicked and piled more on her and sent Earl out in the weather to brave the storm.

Upon Earl's return he'd not only brought with him their tribal sage he brought back as much firewood as the two of them could carry. By the time the fire was kindled Brenda was delirious and struggled to breathe. The Stillwater siblings gathered together and watched helplessly as their baby sister's life ebbed away. When Brenda died they said she looked so serene and at peace that it was easy for them to imagine that she had traveled to her happy hunting ground but that she would always be missed. The harsh winter left the ground frozen and so Brenda's little body was placed in the barn wrapped in a blanket until the soil thawed enough that her grave could be dug.

Come the spring Brenda was laid to rest in their ever expanding family cemetery. Brother Earl was killed later that same year when the walls of the well he was digging collapsed, crushing him under the weight of the earth. Their brother Ray was first on the scene and alerted the rest of the family who came running. Tragically, Earl's lifeless body was recovered but there was nothing more to be done except to rebury him next to his brother Walter.

Mom said that for her, the shock of losing her brother Earl was the worst day in her childhood and that she would never forget her brothers and sisters clawing at the ground with their hands, sticks and shovel desperately trying to rescue him. She said that her brother Earl was young, handsome, and full of what she said was piss and vinegar. Earl was generous with his time and that he had a smile that could light up a room but that he did not take guff from anyone, an attribute she admired. Earl was just seventeen when he died and was the glue that held the rest of the Stillwater children together and so when he went they were broken and began to disperse all over the country.

Mom did not often talk about the loss of her brother Earl except to say how awful the grief was for them all. Within three months of Earl's death brother Carl moved north and was rumored to have taken up with some unsavory members of Detroit's Purple gang but no one knew for sure. Bud too moved away and ended up in Akron, Ohio where he was hired by Quaker Mills. None of them knew where their brother Ray got off to. One day Ray was there and the next he was nowhere to be found. With all the Stillwater boys either dead and buried or just gone, the remaining sisters took their leave and moved away trying their best to leave the bad memories behind them so they could start their lives anew. Florence and Ruby moved to Indiana and lived near Muncie whereas my mom ended up in Pittsburgh and took a job at the local theater. Like mother, father had just moved to Pittsburgh from out of town and was just settling into the area. While mother worked as a ticket agent, father worked at in a nearby factory. From the moment he stepped up to that window to purchase his movie ticket their eyes met and they became a couple and after a whirlwind courtship, they married and before they knew it or were ready for it had started a family of their own. Just shy of their first anniversary mom quit her job at the theater and I came into the frame. Twelve months later my sister Evelyn Louise came along and three years after Evelyn's birth mom and dad had their first son, James Morgan.

My father was in steel, or should I say steel filled his heart but I think it was beer that flowed through his veins. Pittsburgh's steel entrepreneurs, Jones & Laughlin, amassed their great fortunes by operating the plants where my father worked and although we were far from rich, my father earned an above average wage in comparison to the common unskilled laborers who collected a mere pittance for a salary. Mill work was not only arduous it was dangerous. Some of the more repetitive jobs could lull a man into a false sense of security when none was promised. It was the cost of doing business when with one slip up that same job could cost a man his life and oftentimes did. There were a few accidents that occurred at the mill that my father knew about but the details were too graphic for our young ears. Those were the ones father was careful to only share with mother but I could always tell when he'd seen something terrible by his demeanor.

Men working in the mill were hard, honest, gritty fellows that took their lumps without complaint and chose to drink and fraternize to calm their nerves. Dad claimed that all of his mates kept stashes of liquor hidden all over the factory. Within and around the plant prohibition did not count for much and was thought to be a cruel joke instituted by fools without the understanding of what it was like to put their own lives down on the line day after day.

Occasionally, father would forgo bellying up to the bar in one of the illegal gin joints that was still operating despite prohibition and actually come home at a decent hour. On those days, he and mom would sit down after dinner and listen to the radio and talk about their day. The chore of tending after us made mother want to pull her hair out by the roots. While dad served his time in a hot smelly, dangerous factory, mom did her time being stuck in the house with us. It was trying for her to keep up with all the chores and the demands of having a family.

Albeit mothering did not come naturally for our mom, I, on the other hand, took to mischief and mayhem like a duck to water, just like my father. He and I were completely in our element rocking the proverbial apple crate and upsetting mother whether we meant to or not. Between our bad behavior and mother's quick temper the mood around our house could switch faster than light enters a window at dawn and could change dramatically from day to day. When father wasn't around her anger would sometimes be directed towards me. One day she would be pleasant and easy to be around and the next day she would be ready to lash out at the drop of a hat. It sometimes seemed as though a dark cloud would blow in and rest heavily upon her controlling her moods. Mother suffered bouts of depression which took her to places difficult to understand. When our family was small and just the three of us she undoubtedly handled everything alright. For mother having one baby was one thing but having three tugging at her apron strings within a few years of each other was more than she wanted to deal with. Whenever she needed dad to be there for her he was out of reach and even though they were married, in most instances she was very much on her own.

When my baby brother James first came along he was fussy and cried all of the time which frustrated all of us but especially our mom who bore the brunt of the burden. As James screamed mother would pace the floor crying. If she wasn't sticking an unwanted bottle in his mouth she was patting his back or rubbing his tummy trying to satisfy him. Once James would quiet down enough to be rocked in a chair mother would sit down cradling him in her weary arms until they would both fall asleep. Mother tried everything imaginable to get him to stop screaming but nothing seemed to work. Even when he would fall asleep in her arms it would not be long before his sleep was disturbed and his painful cries started again. On the rare occasions baby James would fall asleep, usually towards the end of one of his feedings, mom would breathe a sigh of relief. After a short waiting period mother would slowly get up and tip toe him over to his crib where she would lay him down as gently as possible, careful not to disturb his fragile slumber. Mother would then cover him with the pink blanket she'd crocheted before she knew he would be a boy. According to father, the blanket was a little feminine but it served the purpose in spite of the color. It was a really pretty blanket and I loved how soft it felt to the touch.

One day after mother had taken James to the doctor to see why he cried so often she came home and explained that James was suffering from something called, colic, and that was why he fussed so much. Her explanation fell flat and left me scratching my head. I had a cowlick which made my hair stick up funny in front, but it didn't make me cry and besides that, I was confused as to how James could have "colic," when he was bald. It took some time for James to finally grow out of the crying stage and would nap peacefully in his crib during the day. When that happened mother would like to take advantage of the situation and would declare it was nap time for us all and to make sure we slept she would climb into bed with us.

On one of those occasions while Evelyn, James, and mother were all asleep I could not and was wide awake. It did not take long before I was overheated and bored. Laying there like a lump for what seemed like an eternity I sat up on the edge of the bed to hog the fan. Because of the heat, our mom had placed an oscillating fan next to our bed on the nightstand. The refreshing breeze felt heavenly as I held the hair up off the back of my sweaty neck. Glancing back I could see that Evelyn and mom were sweating comfortably. I began to ponder how our wonderful fan worked because the illusion was that its blades all but disappeared when in operation and that fascinated me. Rhythmically the fan rocked back and forth, back and forth on its base circulating the air while cooling me down enough to think. It seemed like magic and so to satisfy my insatiable curiosity I stuck my finger in through the decorative grill as a kind of test to see if I could stop the motion. Well needless to say my little experiment went terribly awry. Instantly those metal blades that were in fact still there weather I could see them or not, had battered my tiny finger like our butcher grinds suet into our meat causing me to scream out in pain.

When mom woke she flew into action and after a quick smack on my backside with her one hand for doing something so stupid she dragged me into the bathroom with her other hand and ran my hurt and bleeding finger under the tap. Rooting through the medicine cabinet mother pulled out a tiny dark brown bottle complete with the ominous skull and crossbones as part of its labeling. After pulling my hand out from under the tap she doused my finger with the wicked red stuff that burned like fire and stained my skin. The iodine treatment she'd used hurt more than the fan blades had. Most of my hand was stained an awful orange red color and my finger throbbed with pain. The staining made it appear that my finger had been cut to ribbons which scared me and made me cry more. That was when mother ordered me to shut up and stop my sniveling.

"You're going to lose that nail," Mom pointed out as she bandaged what was left of my mangled finger tip.

Worried about how my finger would look without a fingernail frightened me and my nose started to run.

"Will it grow back?" I asked, sniffling.

"Oh, who knows," Mom said, rolling her eyes and then came out with a, "Knock it off, or I'll really give you something to cry about."

I wondered how she could say such a thing. Mom went on to say that what I had done was really stupid, but I preferred to think of it as adventurous firstly and then maybe just a little stupid. It was all relative depending on how you looked at it.

From that day on, I let the fan do its job of keeping us cool during the sweltering summer months and I did my job in heeding mother's warning for me to keep my grubby little paws to myself. No one would ever have to warn Evelyn about what the fans razor sharp blades could do to a finger, my little stunt took care of that and she had me to thank for it. Seeing how the fan blades chewed up my finger Evelyn would not have messed with the fan for all the tea in China. Curiosity was not in her nature. Evelyn was a quiet, mild tempered beauty, touting soft brown curly locks, bright blue eyes with magnificently long lashes. She had chubby, pinch worthy cheeks and thick pouty lips that made her look like a classic Kewpie Doll. After James had outgrown the colic phase he turned into a wonderful baby. Our James was a baldy boy with a bulbous head and a big gummy smile. It took more than a year before his dark wavy hair grew in enough to cover the vast expanse of his huge cranium and another three years before James spoke his first real word. James had curious blue eyes and a radiant smile and was all of our joy.

I often thought that if my mother had ever found and rubbed Aladdin's magic lamp her first wish might have been for great wealth but her second might have been for me to have never been born so she could go straight to having Evelyn and James. It was anyone's guess what her third wish would have been for. If I'd ever found that magic lamp my first wish would have been that our father would always be around and that he came straight home from work which would have made us all happy. My second wish would have been for wealth so dad wouldn't have to work so hard and with those two wishes, I didn't need a third.

As far as I was concerned I was down to earth and not overly sensitive or moody, unlike my sister Evelyn, who seemed to cry over every little thing that happened and was as moody as mother, but I did have to hand it to Evelyn though; she could play mom and dad like a fine tuned fiddle and got her way more often than not. Evelyn had mastered the effective use of manipulation in ways I could only dream of. My actions were always deliberate and usually met with instantaneous consequences. Counting the cost of everything I rarely asked for much. Evelyn, on the other hand asked for everything and whenever possible got what she asked for, which gave credence to my belief that my little sister was nothing more than a spoiled, whinny do-gooder. My big complaint with her was that she tattled on me every chance she got and the way I looked at it, no one needed to rat me out, I could get into enough trouble without anyone else's help. Suspiciously, whenever I'd stick my nose somewhere it did not belong Evelyn was always there to tell mom all about it. Her squealing on my mischief made me look like the devil incarnate, while she was able to portray the perfect little angel.

Evelyn and I bickered often over petty things which at times practically drove mom around the bend. By the time our little brother, James had come along much had changed. We had just moved from a small apartment and into our own home and in some respects; a new life. In the beginning mom and dad were playful and happy again and worked as a team the way parents should.

There was one thing about James that troubled mom after the colic. It took him until he was nearly three years old before he spoke his first words but I though why should he speak, all James needed to do was grunt and point and he got what he wanted, which was pretty simple and it worked. Still I knew it bothered mom that James did not say even the simplest words like, mama or dada for so long. I think she feared there was something seriously wrong with him developmentally but I figured James would talk as soon as he had something to say, and he did.

CHAPTER TWO
PUNCHING RONNY

The Anthony's were a family living next door to us on the block. They, like our family was made up of three children. The only difference between them and us was that they had two boys and a girl, whereas we had the opposite, two girls and a boy. Their eldest boy, Ronny Anthony, was a tall, lanky, bucked tooth boy who stood a head taller than me as he should seeing he was a year older. He had grayish green eyes, sandy blonde hair and a freckly face. I thought he was as mean as a snake and twice as ugly. Ronny's little sister, Susie, was a skinny girl with strawberry blonde hair that was kinky curly. Susie, we found out had more than one unusual quirk. The baby of their family was a scrawny, booger eating boy named Jasper. My sister Evelyn and Susie were good friends. I on the other hand could only tolerate Susie and would play with her on rare occasions.

One day while minding my own business I'd discovered Susie and Evelyn sitting on the ground singing to a spider. Up until then Evelyn had always been terribly afraid of spiders but because Susie claimed that the spider was her pet and that he loved being sung to while building its web Evelyn had overcome her fear and actually participated in Susie's strange ritual of arachnid crooning. Spiders never scared me much but I was never a fan. When I saw the size of that particular one, it frightened even me. It was a large black and yellow spider with long spindly legs crawling all over a huge web suspended in a bush behind Susie's house which made me glad it lived over there and not in our yard. To see the two of them sitting in front of its web singing lead me to believe they were both nuts.

Susie's father was a gruff cantankerous man named, Jack. Mr. Anthony possessed no sense of humor at all and acted like a grumpy old man even though he was just in his mid twenties. Jack Anthony would come home from work and bark out orders like he was the only one in the world with a brain and he demanded absolute obedience from his subordinate's who according to his twisted thinking were his wife and children. Jack's wife Ethel, also known as the local busybody, would pop in to our house on occasion to gossip and fill mom's ears with a lot of nonsense that no one really cared about. The instant Ethel would get wind that her husband might be lurking around she would panic and hightail it home. Once when my sister Evelyn and I were playing a friendly game of Jack's at the Anthony's home, Susie's little brother Jasper came in to pester us, as little brothers often do. Our petty squabble caused big Jack to storm into the room to settle the argument once and for all.

Without warning Mr. Anthony rushed in screaming and snatched Jasper up over his head only to drop him onto the floor in the middle of our game. It was shocking and we were all terrified by the ferocity of the attack. Poor little Jasper got up and scurried off crying with a couple of pointy jack spur's still stuck in his backside. Needless to say, the Jasper/Jack episode abruptly ended our game and stuck in our memories just like the jack spurs had stuck in Jaspers skin. The traumatic event resulted in Evelyn and I going home and Susie racing to the milk shoot where she had stashed a comforting pair of her mother's silky panties earlier. As soon as Susie secured the sateen undergarment she ran outside to hide from her mom's view who did not appreciate what she was up to. Once protected from view, Susie always covered her favorite thumb with the silky fabric and sucked away like there were no tomorrow. The strange obsession satisfied her whenever she became anxious. Susie kept the embarrassing undergarments stashed in various places all over the house so her mother wouldn't find them. Just like my father said the factory workers kept bottles of booze hidden about the factory Susie had a little stash of her own. All of the Anthony's feared what might happen if big Jack ever found out about Susie's strange panty fetish.

The oldest boy in the Anthony brood was Ronny. Now Ronny was one of many neighborhood bullies who liked picking on anyone vulnerable and my sister Evelyn turned out to be one of his favorite targets. When mother informed father about the bullying he came up with a plan on how to put a stop to it. Because Ronny was really just a kid and a neighbor of ours, dad thought it best that a kid should handle the situation and so he appointed me to the job.

I'll never forget the day father filled me in on what he wanted me to do to Ronny. Dad took me out to the shed where after a brief demonstration on how to hit a speedball lifted me up and told me to punch it as hard as I could. My father could make that odd shaped ball sound like a woodpecker boring into the side of a buggy tree trunk with his rolling fist of fury. When I hit that punching bag I thought I broke my knuckles. The speedball was much harder than I expected but father assured me that I'd done alright for my first try and that the next time Ronny Anthony came around harassing Evelyn I should pretend Ronny's head was that ball and punch him as hard as I could. Dad said that if Ronny Anthony ever came into our yard again looking for trouble; trouble was what he would find. Father could see that I was worried about his plan. Ronny was taller and a lot stronger than me and we both knew it. I was just a skinny little girl who barely cast a shadow and

I'd never punched anyone in my life and now my father was counting on me to even the score and duke it out with the bully next door. All sorts of pictures went through my thoughts none of which ended well for me.

All I could think was, what did I care if Ronny picked on Evelyn once in awhile? If my punch failed, Ronny could bend me like a pretzel only to snap me in half. Father tried explaining the concept that the bigger they are the harder they fall but I had my doubts. Father seemed to be placing an awful lot of confidence in me that I wasn't sure I deserved and it only took a couple of days for my worst fears to come true.

Evelyn was in the front yard entertaining James by pulling him around in our little red wagon when Ronny appeared, seemingly out of nowhere. He had decided that he was going to commandeer our wagon and ordered James to get out and lunged at him as though if James did not move fast enough he would be removed by force. With James out of the way and sitting on the ground crying Ronny then turned his attention to Evelyn who was still holding onto the wagons handle. They began grappling for control and I dare say that Evelyn put up a brave fight before Ronny over powered her and shoved her aside like a ragdoll knocking her to the ground causing her to cry. It all happened so fast and without thinking of the consequences I grew a spine and went after Ronny for what he was doing to James and Evelyn.

Because he was walking away with our wagon I was able to catch him completely off guard. I lit on him like a banshee and punched him as hard as I could right in his nose using an uppercut that even James Braddock would have been proud of. As soon as my boney little fist connected with Ronny's freckled nose the blood squirted out like Yellowstone Park's, Old Faithful surprising both of us to no end. Instantly Ronny grabbed his nose and as soon as the shock wore off that a puny little girl like me had taken him down a notch he began bawling his eyes out, dropping our wagon's handle.

It seemed that for Ronny to see his blood spill onto the ground was more than he could stand and the sweet victory was mine. Proudly I bent over picking up the handle from the sidewalk and walked over to Evelyn and James and gave it back to them. With our red bull dog wagon delivered Evelyn and James thanked me for what I'd done and I walked away feeling as big as a mountain and twice as mighty.

Dad was right and his plan worked like a charm. From that day forward Ronny Anthony never messed with us or anything that was ours. When my father came home that evening and heard what I had done to Ronny he was full of pride and told me so. The time I stood up to Ronny Anthony and socked him square in his nose was one of the proudest days of my life and knowing how much it had pleased my dad was a thrill. Every so often father would mention the Rose verses Ronny incident in front of guest and when he did he would be beaming with pride over the bravery his little girl exhibited when she alone took on the neighborhood tough guy. The thought of me slugging Ronny always brought a smile to not only my face, but my father's as well.

CHAPTER THREE
CONTRAPTIONS AND DISASTERS

Growing up in Pittsburgh had its advantages and disadvantages. There were plenty of things to do as long as you could tolerate the ever present shroud of smoky air that sat heavily upon our city. The clouds were so thick at times they could block out the sun at noon. It was like living under an enormous gray elephant teetering awkwardly upon an undersized circus drum. When I was midway through my first year of school mother developed a severe case of double pneumonia. Her illness made her weak as a kitten and so for that reason she took to her bed and was unable to take care of us. When the doctor came around to our house and diagnose the double pneumonia he concluded that the heavily polluted air outside were a huge contributor in weakening mother's lungs and that the likelihood of her recovering was good as long as we allowed her to have complete bed rest.

Because of the severity of the pollutant's outside, mother's flare up was bad and we were ordered to batten down the hatches. After going around the house closing all windows and doors father instructed us that we should be mindful not to run in and out of the house and that we were to stay quiet whenever we were inside as not to disturb mother as she recuperated.

During mother's bout with pneumonia father was amazing and delegated who would do the basic chores. Evelyn and I washed and dried dishes while father put them away. James was in charge of keeping his toys picked up and dad did all the cooking. The food was tastily delicious and we all enjoyed every bite. Dad fried all foods in butter. Of our favorites were things like cheddar cheese, thin sliced green tomatoes, bologna and milk gravy on toast, beans on toast and the likes. While mom was ill dad even mastered the art of preparing us a dessert that he called fried dough and cherries.

After blending his homemade lumpy biscuit batter dad would heat some butter in mom's cast iron skillet and plop his pasty concoction into the pan. Once it browned around the edges dad would spoon in some sweet cherries from a tin into the middle of the pancake and folded the batter over the top like a tart. After it was golden brown and the fruit syrup caramelized around the edges dad would removed the tart from the pan and sprinkled a little powdered sugar atop them to complete his wonderful dish that we enjoyed warm.

The entire time mother was ailing father managed to come straight home from work instead of stopping at a bar for a drink like he usually did. This was a great relief for mother who was pleased by his attentiveness to us in her absence. While father was tending to our daily needs, mother's appetite had waned which left more food for us and we were happy to eat up everything dad set in front of us. It was such a joy to see our father in the kitchen happily singing when he was cooking and cleaning. In order to keep mother's strength up dad insisted she finish at least a cup of broth and a few crackers every day whether she wanted to or not. We loved all the extra attention we were receiving while mom was sick.

During the time mother was confined to her room and because father was such a prankster he decided to amuse himself by having a little fun at my expense. Unsuspectingly father woke me extra early for school insisting he help me get ready. That Friday and after eating breakfast dad took me into the other room and had me to sit on the floor in front of him so he could fix my hair. I'd always done my own hair but because dad really wanted to help I was given no choice but to let him. He began plaiting my hair with an undetermined number of individual braids. When he'd finished he handed me a mish-mash of items to ware, none of which remotely went together, and told me to get dressed.

Feeling silly and looking absolutely ridiculous I was made to go to school where I was teased all day because of the oddity of my appearance. Despite my tears when I came home from school that day father tried assuring me that it was really funny and that one day even I would laugh about it. It was a dastardly prank and I never did believe it to be funny but had to admit that time helped make it seem not so bad.

By the time mother regained her strength from her bout of pneumonia and was able to get back to her normal routine father went back to his normal routine and began stopping off for a drink or twelve after work with his pals. The joke was that for father, one drink was too many and twelve was never enough. It is said that absences makes the heart grow fonder but in their case father's absence made mother's heart towards him grow bitter and their fights over dad spending so much time in the local beer gardens resumed.

Amongst the three Evan's siblings, my brother James was more like me than my sister Evelyn ever was. Despite the fact that we were so close in age and of the same gender Evelyn and I butt heads. James was James, a rambunctious boy that got into all kinds of mischief, just like me and I loved him for it. The only difference between us was that James could get away with acting up where I could not. James was the baby and the first boy and despite his insatiable curiosity mother always stood up for him. He was her blue eyed boy and we all loved him. Being the eldest allotted me some advantages that neither James nor Evelyn had. Theretofore; I learned that my role also bore some disadvantages besides. One of which was that being the eldest I was responsible for setting a standard of behavior where in all reality Evelyn would have been far better suited for the role. Unfortunately, for the two of us, she arrived a year too late and I had already secured the job by default.

Evelyn was an old soul from birth who possessed the innate ability of distinguishing right from wrong at an early age. Without hesitation and regardless of if any adult was present to witness what we were up to Evelyn would inevitably choose the right path and follow it only to squeal on me for veering the other way. In my opinion I thought she was crazy. Between her good sense and perpetual tattling on me she had the knack of making me look bad in our parent's eyes which was something I resented and never understood. Evelyn seemed so hell bent on setting the world right no matter how many times I ended up getting the strap because of it. Evelyn's goody-two-shoes attitude was, in fact, her inherent nature while mine was the opposite.

My personality was more mischievous and sneaky and I liked pushing the envelope no matter how many times I'd been warned against doing it. If I had any sense at all I might have learned my lesson but mischief seemed to draw me like a moth to the flame. Admittedly, I was headstrong and unlike Evelyn who complied too every rule that was set in front of her, I defied them and looked at it as a personal challenge to see how much I could get away with. It seemed to all come down to a war of wills between me and Evelyn and while she was always trying to figure out what kind of trouble I was up too, I was doing my best to stay clear of her prying eyes and ears so I would not get caught doing whatever it was I was dabbling in at the time.

The importance of my position as the eldest of our family was something that I took very serious. A kind of trailblazer for all those that came after me and dare I say that I, Rose Elizabeth Evans, possessed that grand pioneering spirit of old and so as far as I was concerned, Evelyn and James owed me a huge debt of thanks. It was always me who bravely overstepped the mark that no child dare cross and it was all done to test the waters to see what we could or could not get away with. My testing of the proverbial waters became my quest in life although I hated that sickening feeling I had in the pit of my stomach whenever I got caught doing something red handed and so to avoid that I got sneakier so I wouldn't get caught. All the bad habits that I was honing were more of a thorn mother's side than they were in fathers, simply because he wasn't around. Mother was the one that had to deal with our everyday life while father was off working or frequenting and fraternizing in one of his many hang outs. The, "red handed," comment was a reference our mother never used and father only said on occasion out of habit. Mother made it known that it offended her Indian heritage and forbade us from using the term.

The fact that Evelyn and I were at odds much of the time created a lot of tension in our home. It took the birth of our brother James to balance our family out. While Evelyn looked at James as this angelic creature that she could not help doting over I loved him for that impish glint he had in his eyes. I recognized that glint right away and I knew he and I were cut from the same cloth. While Evelyn was like a dainty piece of lace, James and I was more like burlap that could chaff and was abrasive. When James was a baby he had a laugh that was infectious and his grin was a delight to behold. His personality amused us all so much and I never complained when I had to keep an eye on him although I did resent it when I was assigned to watch Evelyn. She and I were practically the same age and so because of that Evelyn would obey anyone except me. James might have been a handful at times but he was so much fun to be around. I loved playing peek-a-boo or any other silly game that would make him explode with laughter and explode he would. His entire body would shake uncontrollably whenever he laughed.

Financially, our family was strapped most of the time and that was despite the fact that father made a decent living down at the steel mill. A good chunk of his time and weekly check was spent frequenting the local bars, taverns and or beer gardens. Despite that dad had managed to equip our house with many of the modern conveniences that mom insisted she needed. Her argument was that if he had enough money to support his boozing and merriment there was certainly enough money to buy the more modern items that could make her life a little easier to which he knew she had a valid point. At mother's insistence we were one of the first on the block who owned an electric wringer washing machine. She'd first seen it featured in the dry-goods stores copy of the Sear's and Roebuck Catalogue. The wringer washer was called "The Mighty Thor," and was manufactured by the Hurley Machine Company out of Chicago. In the picture it showed that it had a galvanized tub, twin wringers and rotating wheels affixed to the legs which made it portable as well as efficient and very desirable for busy women. Mother had to have it and so the washer was ordered and delivered to our house. When it arrived all the neighbors came out to see what we had. It was a proud moment for mother as she directed the delivery man that it was to be set up in our kitchen.

The first time she slid it across the floor, plugged it in and hooked it up to the kitchen sink was a grand day indeed. Mother had us to gather up anything soiled so she could test it out. Our Mighty Thor worked like a dream. Our new electric wringer washer could wring out everything including my baby brother's tiny arm. It was a warm humid day and we'd owned the washer for three months when the accident happened. By then mother seemed to be a professional laundress and would leave the wringers engaged when she went out to hang the damp clothes on the clothesline. As usual and without being told I was to keep an eye on James while mother was busy in the backyard. Evelyn was next door playing with Susie Anthony and so it was just me and James who was otherwise occupied and playing quietly on the floor with his one toy truck. I was sitting at the table drawing a picture and was totally engrossed in my art. The dull swoosh, swoosh noise of the washing machine helped to cover up the sound of James sliding a chair next to the tub so he could get a better look. Being the monkey that he was James then climbed up the chair and pulled his body up to the tub. He must have been fascinated by the movement of the wringers just like I had been fascinated by the blades of our oscillating fan. All it took was for James to touch those rolling pins. The racket he made moaning and thrashing and kicking the galvanized tub caused me to look up and panic. It appeared to me that our Mighty Thor was eating James alive as he hung suspended with his arm caught in the machine. It was horrible and I raced to the side door to scream for help and mother came a running. Frantically she rushed over to James side and flipped the emergency lever atop the machine that separated the rollers enough to free his arm.

It was a frightful experience for us all and mother sat down in the same chair that James had drug over to the machine and cradled him caringly in her arms while wiping away his tears and kissing his forehead to comfort him. As soon as James calmed down enough to have his arm looked over mother gently lifted it as high as James would allow. She asked him to wiggle his fingers to make sure nothing was broken and smiled when he did it letting us all know that he would be alright. His hand and forearm appeared normal but his little armpit had red squiggly lines underneath where the wringers had left their marks. My second worry after James's wellbeing was what mother would do to me for not watching him better but I think mother was so relieved that James was alright, she never scolded me for the unfortunate accident.

Evelyn, James and I would have been a handful for any single parent and although our folks were married, they were rarely a couple. Our mom did her best to be a good parent but it seemed motherhood did not come naturally for her. Frazzled and completely overwhelmed by her difficult role mother often lashed out in fits of temper. I understood she was lonely and sorely missed our father's help, we all missed him. Mom's frustration strained to the point of breaking more times than we could count. She and father suffered horrific fights that were frightening to see and although I'd never witnessed him hit her I did see mom striking dad from time to time. Sometimes their fights were so loud it sounded like a train was crashing through the house. On those occasions Evelyn, James and I would cower under the sheets in our bed sobbing and wishing they would just stop.

Because James was so afraid of the dark our parents would leave our bedroom door ajar which allowed some light to filter in. The three of us slept in the same bed which might have been a tight fit but none of us minded. Whenever one of us would turn over in the bed the other two needed to follow the leader and roll as well. James felt more secure in the middle so that was where he slept, farthest away from the dreaded reach of the crack monster that he believed lived under our bed. Neither Evelyn nor I feared the crack monster so we were alright sleeping on the outer edges of the bed. Evelyn preferred sleeping next to the wall and I guess because I was the oldest and I suppose the bravest, was elected to sleep on the outside nearest the door. If anyone ever came in to hurt us, I would be the one taken.

To entertain myself after James and Evelyn were fast asleep I'd stay still in bed and squint while looking at the shafts of light that seeped in through the crack of our door. By squinting I could create the illusion that I was stretching the beams to new dimensions. Sometimes I'd hear mom and dad playfully teasing each other of which I enjoyed listening to. Their happy banter back and forth made me feel secure in that maybe deep down inside they really did love each other. Then there were the other times when I feared they would kill each other if they did not stop fighting. From my position in bed I had a clear shot of their threatening silhouettes as they moved in and out of the frame brawling throughout the house.

They were tumultuous days to say the least. Often when we came in from playing, mom would be sitting at the kitchen table bawling her eyes out. We may not have always known the reason for her tears but it was assumed it had something to do with our father. Either dad had done something wrong or he'd forgotten to do something right. Regardless of how it all went down we knew who she thought the culprit was behind her sorrow.

On one of mom's more gloomy days, Evelyn and I, hoping to uplift her mood, offered to take James with us so he would not be underfoot. Because she'd been so distraught that particular day she gave us the go ahead and we left with James and went down to the Duquesne Incline to play. After meeting up with a few of our friends we became engaged in a lively game of hide and seek. The game was one of our favorites and there were a number of really good places to duck and hide behind in our neighborhood. Our friend Marcy and I were squatting down near the loading station when Evelyn's friend Susie, the seeker, called out, "olly-olly-oxen-free."

Having heard the "olly-olly call," Marcy and I peeked out to check if the coast was clear and came racing from our cover to our designated home base without fear of being tagged out. During our maneuvering around the tracks, James tripped and took a nasty fall hitting his head on a rock where he laid unconscious on the ground for what seemed like forever. Evelyn and I panicked to see the blood all over his lifeless face. Leaving Evelyn behind I hopped onto Susie's brother's bike and headed for home to fetch mom. As usual dad was no where around and thought to be in some bar smoking a Tom Keene Cigar while knocking down a few pints of ale with his work pals. Mom came running as I lead the way. When mother got there James was awake and ready to play. Mother panted from her run and knelt down next to him and looked into his eyes to make sure he did not have a concussion. She pressed her chore apron over his cut trying to stop the bleeding and sobbed for fear she could have lost him. James was fine but within a week of his accident mom packed some of our belongings an informed us that we were leaving Pittsburgh and dad for good.

We knew she was serious when she waved a bus pass she had in her hand claiming that she had had enough. I had no idea what she meant or where we were going but I did not like the sound of what she was threatening to do. Confused and concerned for how dad would get along without us I begged mom to let me stay behind so I could take care of him but she would have none of it and said something about he made his bed and now he had to lie in it. Together we walked to the depot with suitcase in hand and boarded the bus that very day.

We had two aunts on mother's side that were married and lived just outside Muncie. Aunt Florence and her husband, Uncle Lenard lived on the one side of town and Aunt Ruby who was married to Uncle Warren resided a few miles away. Mom figured that if Florence had any trouble taking us in, Ruby and Warren surely would. The bus ride was a long, agonizing trip and I had no idea where we were headed and worried that I would never see my dad again. Mom cried quietly the entire trip. James was the lucky one. He was far too young to grasp what was going on but Evelyn and I knew what was happening and the two of us stared aimlessly out the bus window hugging our feather tics while wondering what was happening to our family.

Without knowing how dad would manage without us there or what he would do when he got home and found the house empty made me feel sick to my stomach. All I wanted to do was go home and by the time we landed on our Auntie' Florence's doorstep I think she felt like me and wished we'd stayed home too. Weary from the road and exhausted our aunt and uncle showed us where we could sleep. They were none too pleased to see the likes of our miserable faces at their front door but after we were in bed my aunt, uncle and mother sat down to hash out an agreement for our future living arrangements. The following morning while Uncle Lenard was at work Evelyn and I heard my mom and her sister compare the differences of their marriages, hers and Uncle Lenard's verses our parents. Evelyn, James and I sat in the other room as to not disturb them.

We could not help overhearing bits and pieces of some of their conversation. Fragments like, "we should have warned them and they had their own problems." kept surfacing.

Even Aunt Florence was sticking up for dad by stating that in her opinion he wasn't such a bad guy and that so what if he likes to drink who doesn't? She went on to defend that he was a good provider in spite of it all. Evelyn and I were really uncomfortable and kept looking at each other wishing they would stop talking about dad like that but they didn't. While we were there father called for us a number of times on the phone. It sounded as though he was begging for us to come home. After a few weeks of phone arguments and a lot of tears mom considered going back to give their marriage another try and we was ever so happy for their decision. The day we returned home and father met us at the bus station mom and dad hugged and kissed and I imagined fell back in love again. It all seemed new and fresh but like the first time their wedded bliss did not last long and dad went back to his old habits of stopping off for a few drinks before coming home which was a constant irritant during their marriage and so because of it their fighting started all over again.

CHAPTER FOUR
OUT LIKE A LIGHT

Mother was a sound sleeper who hated getting up early. Every chance she could mother would stay in bed until nine or sometimes ten o'clock in the morning. Father always maintained that because she and I were born in the afternoon we were more late owls rather than early birds. I didn't know what that had to do with the price of potatoes but in some strange way it sounded logical and so his simple explanation satisfied me.

Because mother was such a heavy sleeper it was next to impossible to disturb her before she was ready to get up. Dad often complained that a freight train could come crashing through our house and it wouldn't stir her and so one day father set out to prove his point. Giving his theory the acid test dad started rummaging through the kitchen cupboards like a madman while mom slept warm and cozy in her bed.

"Eureka!" Dad exclaimed as he held up a couple of large tin pan lids. After being invited to watch his demonstration father pre-warned us that for safeties sake we should keep our distance in case mom woke up swinging. Evelyn, James and I huddled together in the hall just outside their bedroom door waiting to see what was going to happen next. Courageously dad went in and stood next to his unsuspecting wife and lifted those lids like a musician holds a pair of cymbals. Father glanced over and gave the nod for us to prepare. All our shoulders tensed up and James held onto his blanket as he nervously chewed the silky corner in anticipation. I was prepared to run for my life as dad clapped those lids together just above mother's head. Unable to look away we waited for the explosion thinking mother would go mad but despite the loud clanging noise mother's only reaction was to roll over and angrily pull the covers up over her head in an attempt to drown out the irritating sound. Dad chuckled for a second and walked out of the room claiming that thus he had rested his case before tossing the pot lids into the sink and walking out the door to go to work.

As usual, I was left in charge of keeping Evelyn and James quiet until mom did get up but after father's little demonstration I realized we could do most anything we wanted and it would not have disturbed her. If we became hungry before she woke I knew how to take care of the situation. We always had a fresh bottle of milk delivered from our milkman and usually there was a box of Kellogg's Cornflakes in our pantry. If the cereal was gone a couple of moon pies would suffice to stave off our grumbling tummies.

Mom slept on her stomach with her face buried so far into her pillow it often left odd crisscrossing sleep furrows embedded deeply throughout her brow and cheek. Eventually the ruts would fade away but it could take hours for them to fully disappear. Whenever mother went to bed angry over something father had or had not done her sleep would be disturbed and she would restlessly kick the mattress repetitively all through the night. Her rhythmic foot thumping over and over again resembled that of an African native sounding an alarm on his war drum. That dull pounding sound was loud enough to seep through the walls and into our bedroom which was adjacent to theirs. Personally, I found the constant thud, thud,

thud, of her jimmy-leg kind of soothing. It reminded me of a grand pendulum clock, tick-tocking away the hours and ironically, like a pendulum clock; I was pretty certain that if mother had her druthers she would have loved to have clocked dad for the way he repeatedly "ticked" her off.

There was at least one memorable occasion when I believe mother retaliated and got her revenge although neither of them ever admitted what probably happened. We were young and in bed fast asleep, us in our room and they in theirs when dad let out an abrupt shout in the night and the next morning father touted a shiner. Dad insisted that mother was sleepwalking and that she came around the foot of their bed and punched him in the eye and then walked back around and laid down again pulling the covers up over her like nothing had happened. Dad swore that when she hit him she had a blank look in her eyes. However it happened the bruising around dad's blackened eye lasted a couple of days. Their entire story sounded screwy to me but dad insisted that it happened just like that and mother claimed she had no recollection of it at all. Whether she did or didn't remember doing it I'm quite sure she at least felt a smidge of satisfaction despite their lame explanation about father's black eye.

Like mother I too enjoyed sleeping in but I always managed to get up for school no matter what. There was that one time when I faked being ill so I wouldn't have to go to school. On that particular day I was extra tired. Mom and dad had been squabbling all night which made me nervous and unable to sleep. By the morning our house was still and dark and my warm cozy bed felt so inviting I devised a plan that I thought might work. After going to the medicine cabinet I took out the thermometer and ran the tip of it under hot water and then sat atop our furnaces heat vent. As soon as I couldn't take the heat anymore I grabbed the thermometer and stood alongside mom complaining to be sick. When she felt the heat coming off me and without even looking at the thermometer mother gave me permission to return to bed. My little ruse had worked like a charm and I was pleased with myself as I went back to our room and crawled into the warm bed alongside Evelyn and James and fell back to sleep. When Evelyn and James got up, so did I but because I'd not gone to school that morning was ordered to stay in my room for the day. That was when I realized my plan was flawed and wished I had not faked being ill no matter how tired I was.

The next day I was eager to get up and go to school. Two of my classmates, Timmy and Tommy Buckhorn who were my school's only identical twins asked why I had been absent and so I told them I'd been ill. I'm not certain why they bore such animosity against me but I found that they did.

Later that afternoon our teacher, Miss. Landers, announced she needed to leave the room for a few minutes and instructed us to stay in our seats until her return. Without thinking much about it and while minding my own business Timmy and Tommy pointed out that I had carelessly left my good sweater lying on the window sill and that the window was open. Their observation made me nervous. They kept goading me by making wild claims like a raccoon might come by and steal it which caused me to believe they might be right. I began fidgeting in my chair and looking over at the window and my sweater.

My grandmother had knitted that sweater for me and if anything happened to it I would be in big trouble. Timmy and Tommy could see that I was nervous about it and so at their insistence I got up from my chair and retrieved my precious sweater and got back to my seat before Miss Landers came back. Upon her return Timmy and Tommy sat up tall in their chairs dancing around like they would wet their pants if she did not call on them soon. I knew the gig was up and I slouched low in my chair with a sinking feeling about what they were going to tell her and I was right. The two of them were about to rat me out.

"Yes boys, what is it ?" she asked rolling her eyes.

"Rosie got out of her chair," Timmy gleefully squealed while pointing at me.

"Yeah, yeah she did," Tommy confirmed excitedly.

Now I had seen that same disapproving look in my mother's eyes a hundred times before but I'd never seen it directed at me from my teacher. Upon hearing that I had disobeyed her direct order Miss. Landers swooped down on me like a hawk snatches a mouse out of the field. She dragged me up in front of the entire class and it was awful. Terrified I stood there and with fire in her eyes when she ordered me to assume the position. I knew what she meant as I'd witnessed the example before. Knowing what was coming I grabbed hold onto the corners of her desk. Even before the swat connected to my backside I began to cry. It was a mortifying experience that was not yet over as my teacher scribbled out a note for me to take home and give to my parents for their signature. My bottom was sore and my pride was bruised but the shame felt the worst. As I walked back to my seat and passed Timmy and Tommy I could see that they were quietly laughing and poking each other which gave me a mind to punch them in their nose like I had punched Ronny Anthony but I stopped myself knowing that Miss. Landers would clobber me for sure for unladylike conduct so I bit my tongue and took my seat.

The four block walk home was the longest of my life and it felt as though I was walking to my death without benefit of a last request. That day was turning out to be the longest day of my soon to be snuffed out life. During the walk home my troubled mind ran through every case scenario of what my parent's reaction would be when I handed them the note. There was no escaping the inevitable, it had to be done, signed and returned to Miss. Landers the next day if I lived that long. Gently I opened the door and held my breath as I tiptoed over and set the folded note on the table. I'd hoped I could get to my room before mother, who was washing dishes at the time, turned around.

"Your late," she said still facing the sink.

"I know, I'm sorry," I said wanting to go to my room.

"What kept you?" she asked.

Taking a big gulp I stood there for a second trying to come up with an answer when she turned around to face me.

"Cat's got your tongue?"

Without knowing what I should do I pointed to the note on the table. "What's this," she asked wiping her wet hands on her chore apron before touching the paper.

Silently she read what Miss. Landers had written. Mother's expression went from curious, to furious.

"Rosie! What did you do now?" she said, demanding an explanation.

That was when I told her about how Timmy and Tommy and how they had coaxed me to get up and then told on me for doing it. To my great surprise and relief mother understood and went so far as to say that it was their fault and that they should have been the ones paddled and not me. Afterwards mother signed the note never divulging what had happened to me at school to father nor did we have any further discussion about it.

Later that same school year I received my second paddling by Miss Landers. That time there was no denying who was at fault. Trying to be clever I'd repeated something that I should not have. The humiliation of that experience was offset by the popularity my bawdy antics had gained me. Even Timmy and Tommy seemed entertained and impressed with my rude comment so much so they tried to befriend me, but I was not interested in their friendship. I'd never forgiven them for the way they tricked me out of my chair only to tattle on me causing me to receive my first lesson in corporal punishment.

The day prior to my second paddling at school my father and I were out running some errands. Father had the intention of building mother a proper shelf so she could display the vast array of bric-a-brac that she'd been collecting over the years. When father offered to take me with him to the local lumber yard I jumped at the chance and hopped into the car.

Sometimes when we were alone dad would let me steer the car which was great fun. It was always a treat for me to be alone with my father.

Our pleasant summer's afternoon had started off on such a lovely note I'd hoped it would never end. The dusty dirt road wound pleasantly through the tree lined hilly countryside. Dad broke out in song and between the invigorating breeze and father's little ditty about some sweet gal who was five foot two, with eyes of blue our carefree afternoon came to an abrupt stop when a lady riding a bicycle unexpectedly crossed our path and rode out in front of us from behind a tree. Father and I both saw the woman at the same time. She seemed to appear out of nowhere and we both let out a scream for her to look out. Instantly father slammed on the footbrake and pulled the handbrake simultaneously while jerking the steering wheel sharply to avoid hitting her.

His evasive move kept us from running her over but the loose gravel caused the car to fishtail wildly until we were abruptly stopped when our car slammed into a tree. It was a frightening experience for all three of us – myself, dad and the lady on the bicycle. It was a miracle no one was badly hurt. As the dust settled we all caught our breath until the tree that turned out to be a Black Walnut, dislodged its load and began pelting dad's car with its gnarly bounty. The sound of those nuts hitting the metal of dad's precious car was shockingly reminiscent of machine gun fire in a gangster movie. The angry look on my father's face grew more intense with every dinging pop, pop, pop those rock hard hulls created and dad began cursing up a storm.

The woman that caused the crash must have realized that my father was not very pleased and after righting her bike hopped on and rode off peddling like there was no tomorrow. Father was furious with her for leaving the scene like she had but I couldn't blame her knowing I'd have done the same. I'd never seen my father so angry as when those nuts started dropping. As soon as the coast was clear dad jumped out of the car still cursing at the woman and calling her all sorts of names that I'd never heard before. While dad walked around the vehicle kicking the ground and assessing the damage counting the pockmarks I got out and started gathering the downed nuts using my dress as a tote. Fortunately the car bumper had done its job and had only suffered a minor dent from where it hit the tree but there were countless numbers of teeny tiny dings all over our car's hood, trunk and roof. When father asked what I thought I was doing I told him that we shouldn't let them go to waste.

Black walnuts were delicious and although our method in getting them to fall from the tree may have been unconventional they were everywhere and ours for the taking. There were enough black walnuts to last us the year. Usually their hulls were next to impossible to penetrate but because most of the nuts had bounced off our car from the high branches some of them had split open making accessing their tasty meaty nut that much easier to enjoy.

Dad must have seen the logic in what I was doing too and gave me the go ahead to pick them up. He even handed me an old gunnysack that he kept in the trunk so I wouldn't stain my dress and get into trouble with mother. For dad, building the shelf had lost its appeal but we carried on and went to the lumberyard despite our accident and picked up the supplies he needed. The drive home was absent of the joyful singsong we'd enjoyed before our accident. When we got back to the house mom questioned why it took us so long and asked about her shelf?

Still upset over the accident father tossed the gunnysack of nuts into the kitchen sink stating, "there's your damn shelf," before walking out the side door in disgust. Without understanding the situation mother followed him back out to the driveway and I followed them both. Dad had gone to the woodshed to retrieve his rubber mallet as I slipped into the backseat of the car where I reached around the floorboards gathering a few loose nuts that had gotten away. As soon as father returned from the shed she started questioning him about the little divots in the bodywork. Father was all too happy to tell her about the, "dumb broad," that caused them. When I asked what, dumb broad meant he defined it for me claiming it was a, "stupid ass woman." Mother did not appear happy with him swearing in front of me but could see how upset he was and did not correct him over it. Dad stayed outside most of the night using a rubber mallet to bump out the pockmarks.

While dad took care of the bodywork in the driveway we started in on shelling all those fabulous nuts. Mom insisted that the hulls and shells were too hard for us to crack and so she took on that job herself explaining it took a certain finesse to do the job right and that she was raised shelling nuts. That was when dad chirped in from the driveway that she was raised splitting hairs not nuts; to which mom shouted out a joking," Ha, ha, very funny," breaking the tension.

Because black walnuts were such a rare find and shelling them reminded her of her youth the chore seemed to lift mother's mood as the job became a family affair. After she peeled off the thick hulls and gave the nuts a light smack with a rock she'd pass them to Evelyn and I to dig out the meat trying to keep the nuts as intact as we possibly could. A few we got out whole but most split in half which was still good. Because James did not want to be left out, mother appointed him the job of disposing of all the discarded shells and hulls. Within two minutes of starting James changed his mind about helping us and went out to see if he could help father instead.

Evelyn caught me eating a few of the nuts and promptly squealed on me. There was no denying I'd eaten some as I could taste the nutty bits still stuck between my teeth. When mom began to scold me over it I claimed it was my finder's fee and surprisingly she agreed but told me the fee had been met and that the rest of the nuts would be used for baking. Happy with her answer we went back to the task at hand. What few I had tasted really good but I took heed to mom's warning and didn't eat another.

We worked for hours shelling those walnuts until all of our fingers were rough and stained black. Afterwards mom scrubbed our hands raw but some of the stains were still visible around our nails and embedded into our fingerprints and remained that way when I attended school the next day. Everything was going fine and I was sitting respectively quiet with my hands in my lap until Miss. Landers announced what the word for the day would be.

"Broad."

I couldn't believe my luck and without thinking I instinctively raised my grubby little black paw in response to the question. Finally I knew the meaning of one of the words and after being called upon by our teacher I blurted out my father's definition with an enthusiastic, "Broad, a stupid ass woman!"

The uproar created by my answer was instantaneous and for a millisecond I thought about standing and taking a bow but my comedic ability to entertain my fellow classmates was short lived and my, "broad" grin soon melted away when I saw the look of horror on our teachers face and my rapturous moment was over.

There she stood, stupefied and appalled holding one hand over her chest as though she were about to have a heart attack and the other hand over her mouth in unbelief of what I had just said. Her shock then turned to rage and she flew at me to drag me back up in front of the class by the shorthairs in front of my left ear. Again I was asked to assume the position and I received my three swats and another note to take home.

When I handed mother the second note she was not as understanding of my latest misdeed as she was with the first one but she did place some of the blame on father for using the derogatory comment in front of me. It was just dumb luck that word of the day turned out to be what it was. The punishment for my faux pas was another licking by her with a wooden spoon and then she came up with a new torture to teach me a lesson. After returning from the pantry with our mason jar of popcorn mother poured a pile of kernels onto the linoleum in the corner of the kitchen and made to kneel on them and wait for my father to come home.

Mom confronted dad immediately with, "do you know what your daughter did today?"

Even if dad had been completely sober, I doubted that in his wildest dreams he could have guessed what I'd done. Then she handed him the note and told him that it was only right that he sign his name since he was the one that gave me the definition. That was when I was dismissed and sent to bed so they could argue. When I got up the next day I found the signed note sitting on the kitchen table. From then on I made sure to mind my P's and Q's and was very careful never to act up in school again.

Although my personality was more like my father, there was no denying I was my mother's daughter. Even when I was little I looked just like the woman in every way. We both had the same button nose, almond shaped green eyes and a well defined mouth. Dad admitted that I had mother's mouth, minus her viper-gated tongue while mother complained that I was my father incarnate.

Whenever I'd been caught doing something wrong or inappropriate; the first thing out of mom's mouth would always be the comparison between me and my father and although she meant it as a slight against my character I could not help but to take the observation as a compliment. I was always proud of my father and loved him very much despite his flaws which in my eyes were few but according to mother were too numerous to count. Though it may have been worded a number of ways the threats all meant the same.

"Just you wait till your father gets home," or "Look what your daughter did," would be her refrain whenever I disappointed or was in trouble. The way she talked, one would think that she bore no responsibility for my existence and that father had me all by himself. Of her two main threats the first was the more troubling because it was anyone's guess when dad would come home . He could walk through the door any minute or it could take hours and I hated having my life put on an indefinite hold. Mother hated the wait too and the longer we would sit counting the minutes for him to come through the door the angrier she'd become and the louder the fight would turn.

CHAPTER FIVE
MY FRIEND, JEFF

The first time I met Jeffery Donald Davis was a day like any other except for the fact that it would be the day that I met the finest person I would ever known excluding my father. It was a Monday morning and as usual I had slept a little longer than I should have and was rushing around the house like a headless chicken trying to get ready for school. With no time to spare I ran the bristle brush lightly through my hair which left the bulk of the nightly matted tangles undisturbed. For breakfast I grabbed a convenient moon pie from the pantry and wrestled its cellophane wrapper open. After grabbing the leather cinch I used to hold my books I raced out the door and while shoving a big chunk of the half opened moon pie into my mouth wished I had time for a glass of milk to help wash it down. The chocolaty marshmallow cake was dry and it caused me to cough and spray out a few of its sweet cracker crumbs.

It was exceptionally warm that day and I remember hearing some thunder rolling in the near distance and I hoped that I could make it to class before the rain started. Up ahead of me I spotted a new kid I'd never seen before strolling along lackadaisically as if he had all the time in the world with no concern that it was about to rain. Even though he was a full city block ahead of me I was able to catch up to him quickly. He looked to be about my age, maybe a little older, but not much. Because of his age and his lack of enthusiasm I felt certain he too was on his way to school and warned him that he needed to hurry along or he would be late. Together we picked up the pace and rounded the corner entering the schoolyard just before the rain and our general assembly was called.

Our teacher stepped out onto the porch and rang her bell while the new kid and I chatted for a minute at the back of the queue. He kindly pointed out that I still had some moon pie remnants on my cheek for which I thanked him with a silent nod as we shuffled single-file into class. Miss. Landers pulled the new kid to the side so she could make the introductions to the rest of her students. While the new boy was made to stand in front of her desk facing us, Miss Landers cleared her throat to get our attention squelching the underlying whispers that were floating around the room about the boy and where'd he come from. The kid, we were told was named Jeffery Davis and he looked terrified to be standing there. Our teacher completed the announcement and instructed us to welcome him to our school which we did with a resounding, "Good morning Jeffery."

When we shouted out his welcome his neck and face turn all blotchy and red. With his seat assigned our teacher turned to prepare for our first lesson. Awkwardly Jeffery walked to the other side of the room to take his chair but when he passed the twins Timmy stuck his foot out to trip him. Jeffery caught himself and only stumbled slightly but we could all tell that the stunt not only embarrassed him it made him angry. Jeffery appeared to be what we called dirt- poor. The clothes he had on were wrinkled and untidy and while his one shoe was completely worn through at the toes his other shoe had a flapping sole when he walked. My father always called them talk-back shoes because they looked like they were speaking to you when they flapped.

Timmy and Tommy Buckhorn were our class clowns and trouble makers. I thought about squealing on Timmy for tripping the kid but stopped myself figuring, why stick my neck out. It was a new year and I had not been in trouble yet but I could see that Timmy and Tommy were going to be a problem for Jeffery.

That first day after the storm had gone through the class was sent outside for recess. The ground was wet and there were puddles all around. Watching Timmy and Tommy move in on Jeffery was like witnessing a pride of lions singling out a weaker prey. Tommy had found a small black snake slithering through some standing water and picked it up. While Timmy distracted Jeffery his cohort brother dropped the snake down the back of the new kid's shirt making all the girls scream, including me.

As the wet reptile writhed around trapped within his shirt Jeffery pulled down the bib straps from his trousers and started ripping off his shirt. All the commotion had riled the snake up good and so as the viper hit the ground it coiled as though it would strike.

By that time Jeffery was past embarrassment and was sorely irritated. Without fear Jeffery snatched up that black racer by its head and took off running to exact revenge. Up until then the Buckhorn's had been doubled over laughing about their prank but the pair panicked when they saw the tables had been turned.

While backed into a corner Timmy and Tommy began begging for Jeffery to stop but their pleas did them no good. Trapped like the rats they were Jeffery shoved the writhing serpent's head into Tommy's screaming mouth declaring that if he liked snakes so much he should kiss one. Timmy tried to get away but Jeff was too fast for him and grabbed him by the collar and shook him like he was a ragdoll before making him too kiss the snake.

I'd always hated snakes and still do but that day on the playground I was able to put my fears aside and watched with great pleasure as Timmy and Tommy got their just desserts. For once their taunting was their own undoing and they were the ones sniveling and crying for a change. Miss Landers came out ringing her bell signaling our recess was over.

Timmy and Tommy shook off what had just happened and after wiping away their snot and tears on their shirt sleeves stood at the back of the line. Jeffery released the black snake which appreciatively slithered off into the tall grass never to be seen again, before going back inside. No one said a word as we shuffled past our teacher and took our seats. Timmy and Tommy were still visibly shaken but neither of them were about to say anything. They were the ones that started the show and it took the new boy to put them back in their place which he had done in grand style. When Jeffery walked past Timmy and Tommy he lunged at them as though he still had the snake in his hand and they both about jumped out of their skins. We all thought it hilarious but nobody laughed out loud we only snickered quietly behind our hands knowing that what had happened behind the schoolyard would be our little secret. Miss. Landers may have suspected something untoward had taken place during our recess by the shouting but she never let on and we returned to our lesson without being questioned about it. The new kid had gained my absolute respect and I felt beholden to him for what he'd done. It was a wonderful day and I felt avenged and satisfied.

When I arrived home that day and told my parents about the brave new boy with the bright blue eyes that had taken on the school bullies my father offered an invitation for him to come by our house. When father heard the boy's last name was Davis he said it was a Welsh name and that we Welsh always stick together. Dad asked if the young man preferred being called Jeff or Jeffery and I shrugged not knowing.

The next morning I waited for Jeffery to pass our house on his way to school and I came out to walk with him. He didn't look back or even slow down until I shouted out, "Hey Jeff wait up!"

My familiarity immediately got his attention and by the time I caught up to him he was grinning broadly and we walked and talked the rest of the way. I asked him which name he preferred, Jeff or Jeffery and he smiled again claiming that he like the sound of Jeff better and so from then on that was what I always called him. I told Jeff that my name was Rose but that everyone except my father called me Rosie. Jeff was pleased when I told him what my father had said about his Welsh heritage and that he was more than welcome in our home anytime. Thrilled with the invite Jeff came around after school that day to meet my parents. My father was yet to come home and my mother was busily sorting out some laundry when we walked in. After the introductions were made I explained that Jeff was the boy I'd talked about. Mother stood up and apologized for the state she was in but pointed out that our laundry did not do itself and went back to the task at hand.

My brother James was kneeling on the floor entertaining himself playing with a block truck that father had made for him. As soon as he saw Jeff standing in our kitchen he invited him to play with him and held up the truck. Jeff smiled and knelt down to James's level and after sliding the wooden truck back and forth across the floor a few times which amused James to no end Jeff stood up saying he needed to leave so his parents wouldn't worry. James was disappointed by Jeff's announcement and so was I.

"Ah, can he stay for supper?" I asked.

"Yeah, mom, can he?" James inserted.

"You heard the boy. He needs to go," mom answered apologetically while glaring at me for daring to open my mouth in front of company without consulting her first.

It was embarrassing and I knew better than to press my luck any further. I saw Jeff out the door and kept my fingers crossed that my mom wouldn't yell at me until after Jeff was out of earshot. Mom explained that under no uncertain terms was I ever to put her in that position and that if and when she wanted to invite someone into our house for supper she would be the one making the offer and not me.

Father came home late that night and a fight ensued. It had been a long day and would prove to be an even longer night. Their screaming kept all of us up until all hours and it was difficult to get up the next day but I did manage. My parent's arguing was not something I liked to talk about. In fact I never told anyone about it until I confided in Jeff about the turmoil on our way to school. Jeff listened and promised me that he would never repeat anything I'd said and I knew he meant it. Together we walked to and from school most every day. On the days we were allowed to play after school we hung out then too. Jeff was a head taller than me and extremely good looking. His clothes might have been ragged and torn but his personality was intact and his company joyful and I was proud to have him as my friend.

CHAPTER SIX
THE PREMONITION

My new friend, confidant and vindicate was a much treasured find indeed and as our relationship flourished Jeff and I became inseparable. Altogether we were so close we shared everything personal and otherwise including some bouts with pinkeye and impetigo. Our occasional outbreaks that we passed to each other were an annoyance but they paled in comparison to the time he, I and nearly a third of our classmates came down with a terrible bout of the hard measles. That contagion took everyone by surprise and everyone that had come down with symptoms was ordered to stay home. Jeff didn't know that I was infected and I didn't know that he was as we were ill simultaneously. Because of my illness I'd been confined to what my mom referred to as, "the poxie-cot." Now the poxie-cot was set up during emergencies to separate the sick from those who didn't need to get sick.

The first four days were brutal and I suffered with a high fever, sore throat, aching chest and a red rash. In order to contain my contamination I was made to sleep on an old army cot, dubbed, "the poxie-cot," that was set up in the far corner of our bedroom where I remained throughout the duration of my illness.

On the forth night of my ailment a terrible thunderstorm rolled through Pittsburgh stirring up the wind and the rain. It was around 3:30 am when the first big lightning bolt hit nearby and lit up our bedroom as though someone was standing in the hallway taking photographs. The lightning was soon followed by a loud clap of thunder that shook the house and rattled the windows. It woke all of us up with a start and brought mom and dad scrambling into our room to make sure we were alright. The noise had James curled up in a ball crying and Evelyn laying wide eye and nervous when they came in and so mother picked James up assuring that everything was alright and began carrying him back to their bed. Evelyn asked if I could come and sleep with her, which would have been fine with me, but mother insisted that I was to stay put. With everyone settled down and James in bed with mom and dad our front doorbell started ringing wildly as if someone was in a panic to get in.

"Who the hell could that be?" Father mumbled as he walked down the hall but when he peeked outside there was no one there and dad went back to bed scratching his head.

"Well, who was at the door?" I could hear mother ask.

"Nobody."

"What do you mean Nobody, somebody rang the bell?" mother questioned.

"Nope, Just what I said, nobody was there, now go back to sleep."

With James tucked in between them resting comfortably mother rolled over and faced the wall worried. She couldn't shake the feeling that the doorbell ringing was another one of her premonitions and feared the worst. For mother it usually brought death when there was an unexplained knock or bump in the night. Her first experience with a premonition was when she was a girl and had heard a distinct knock on the wall the night before her mother died during childbirth.

The same thing happened with an unexplainable knock that occurred the day prior to her father's passing and again when her brother Earl was buried alive while digging that well. All these deaths were preceded by unexplained noises and so mother was bound to take this occasion and the ringing of our doorbell very seriously.

By the next morning my fever broke and I was starting to feel better but because mother seemed agitated and disconnected she made me to stay in the cot for another day. As soon as she got breakfast out of the way she sent James and Evelyn out to play. The house was quiet and calm. I was still feeling weak and puny and so while mother carried on with her chores I napped and was resting soundly only to be awakened by the joyful shouts of my mom. It was then that I realized her long lost sister, our aunt, whom we had not seen in years, had surprised us with an impromptu visit and was standing on our stoop.

They were ecstatic to see each other again and positively giddy with excitement as she welcomed Ruby into the house. Mother's behavior was reminiscent of bubbly schoolgirl instead of the stern disciplinarian that I was a custom too. From my cot I could hear their tearful reunion and watched as they walked arm and arm down our hall and into the kitchen. One of the first things mother brought up was how our doorbell rung the night before signaling that something big was about to occur and how relieved she was that it was good news for a change and not that someone she loved had died. Ruby chuckled commenting that she was glad she wasn't dead too.

It had been nearly three years since they were last together and they had a lot to catch up on. We'd never got to see our Aunt Ruby when we made our last awful trip to Indiana a few years prior and mother was absolutely thrilled by her sister's company and could hardly contain herself. Mother giggled as she rinsed the dregs from her earlier brew and dumped the used grounds into the trash and started a fresh pot. As their coffee brewed on the stove the two of them sat down and began chatting up a storm. Enhancing their conversation was sound of the coffee pot rhythmically percolating in the background with its heavenly aroma seeping into my room. The shock of seeing her sister's face after such a lone time made mother to forget all about me and I was glad for it.

From my position I could see and hear everything that was going on and so I kept my mouth shut. The entertainment was a grand diversion and it wasn't until my stomach rumbled with some serious hunger pains that I feared might blow my cover but they hadn't. It had been five days since I'd eaten anything besides a few saltine crackers and some chicken broth but my appetite would have to wait, this was far too amusing and everything was perfect. Father was off at work. Evelyn and James were somewhere outside playing and I had slipped under mom's keenly honed radar and felt well enough to appreciate the front row show of their reunion and I could not believe my luck for being sick that day. My aunt Ruby turning up on our stoop was nothing short of miraculous as it cured my headache, hunger and even my sore throat became tolerable.

Mother was always going on about how beautiful her sister Ruby was and that her name described her persona to a tee and it seemed that as soon as she entered our house her healing power began working for both me and mother. It was as though radiant beams of light emanated from her being and I had to agree with mom when she said our Aunt Ruby was something to behold.

Mom poured them each a cup of coffee and grabbed something from the refrigerator for them to snack on. It looked so good and as soon as I saw the plate of food placed on the table my tummy gave out another rumble and so I pinched it hard to make it stop. Mom made comment that Ruby must be starved from her exhausting trip in which almost made me laugh thinking, "what about me, don't you think I might be a little hungry too?" but I of course kept my mouth shut.

Aunt Ruby admitted she was famished and nibbled on a bit of something from off the plate as she rehearsed the horror story that was her bus ride into Pittsburgh. She laughed about how the bus was hotter than hell and that it smelled something awful. Aunt Ruby claimed that there were a couple of, "brats," aboard fidgeting the entire trip and that their mother should have been slapped for letting them run around like a couple of wild Indians. Then Aunt Ruby started in on some man that was sitting in front of her on the bus claiming he was as big as a house and was touting the worst toupee she'd ever seen in her life. Aunt Ruby said his hairpiece was so bad it flopped over his face every time his head dropped to his chest as he fought off his urge to sleep. Laughingly she said it looked like he had a dead rat atop his head. Her graphic comparison made them both laugh so hard that mom begged her sister for mercy as she doubled over wiping the tears from her eyes. After regaining their composure the subject turned to a more serious note and mom questioned why she had not given her fair warning that she would be coming into town.

Aunt Ruby apologized with the explanation that it was a last minute sort of thing that could not be helped. Ruby said she'd missed mom's advice and confessed that without it she had made some bad decisions that she believed mother could have spared her from.

When mother asked what she was referring to their conversation dropped to a whisper and I couldn't catch all of what was then said. With the whispering over and while sipping their coffee and snacking on the cheese and crackers Ruby complained about her marriage being in shambles. Mother asked if her husband, Warren, had found out about someone named Ralph when Aunt Ruby confessed that he was suspicious and that during a fight over it had knocked her down after which she'd packed a valise and hopped the first bus heading for Pittsburgh to see mom. Mother was outraged that Warren had put his hands on her but Ruby said it was nothing and that she was just teaching him a lesson. That was when the subject got really juicy and they lowered their voices again. Keeping as still as I could on my poxie-cot I pulled the covers up tightly around my chin and I was able to get the "gist" of what was being said but some of it went right over my head. Aunt Ruby made a comment that Warren was so soft it was like sticking a marshmallow into a piggybank slot which when it was said mother practically fell out of her chair and started laughing hysterically.

The name Ralph Crossman kept creeping into their conversation and it took me awhile to figure out that while Warren was her husband, Ralph was more than a friend to Ruby. At first I thought Mr. Crossman made deliveries or was a linoleum installer because Aunt Ruby kept saying he came around every chance he could and that he was really a good lay.

Mom asked if either Ralph or Warren knew where she was and warned her that she was playing a very dangerous game that mother wanted no part of. Ruby promised that neither knew where she was and mom told her to keep it that way.

By the time James came running into the kitchen complaining that he was starving the subject had changed and was lighthearted. James stopped dead in his tracks when he saw a stranger sitting at the kitchen table big as life. Ruby commented on how handsome he was and that he would be a real lady killer when he grew up. Mom made the introductions and told James he would have to hold his horses about eating and that she would be fixing something for us all shortly. Not long after that Evelyn came in to use the toilet and again Ruby marveled by commenting on how pretty she was and that she belonged in the movies. Then our aunt asked about me and where I was?

"Oh shit! I forgot all about Rosie," mom said jumping up from the table.

I saw her coming and so I pretended that I was just waking up and gave a big yawning stretch, rubbing my eyes when she entered the room. Mom felt for signs of a temperature by placing the back of her hand on my forehead and was relieved to know that I was normal, or at least that my fever had not returned. When I complained that I was really hungry she said that was a good indication and gave me permission to get out of bed and come join them in the kitchen. As I got up Evelyn came rushing in wanting me to guess who our visitor was and that I would never believe it. Mom concurred that indeed we did have a surprise guest to which I acted dumb.

It felt really good to throw off the blanket and get up from the cot but initially I went all giddy in the head and when I first stood up my legs went all rubbery. As I made my way to the kitchen I sat down at the table and laid my head down. My long lost aunt greeted me with a welcoming smile and an unwitting chuckle. When mother saw my head down she snapped at me, "Hey, if you're that tired go back to bed, nobody wants to see that."

The unsympathetic suggestion made me to sit up and act as though I felt fine although I didn't really. It had been a week since I'd looked into a mirror and I was well aware that I looked the sight. At the time even my hair hurt. My once wavy brown locks had twisted and turned into a wadded up matted mess that wasn't fit to stuff a mattress. My head had taken on an odd flat shape that must have resembled a mangy lion's mane. The red blotches that covered my body had diminished but were still visible. Because I'd not eaten in a few days it appeared that I had lost a few precious pounds that I could not afford to lose. Father always teased me that I was skinnier than a rake handle and because of that couldn't cast a shadow. My frightful state probably gave Aunt Ruby the thought that the only movie I could have played a role in would have to have been some kind of horror film and even there I might have given Lon Chaney a run for his money but I didn't care I was just glad to be out of bed.

When mother suggested that she would make a batch of something we called "Rivel's," Aunt Ruby was thrilled. She had not had Rivel's since she and mom were kids and was anxious to have some. Rivel's were an old family recipe. They consisted of tasty little egg dumplings that were cooked in slow boiling water with thick sliced potatoes. Ingredients for the dumplings were all purpose flour, whole eggs, salt and pepper. When the gooey batter was mixed it was scooped from the bowl with the tip of a teaspoon and plopped into the pot of hot water to cook alongside the sliced potatoes until done which only took about fifteen minutes. After that the water was drained and the potatoes and dumplings were returned to the pot with the addition of some milk, butter and a bit more salt and pepper to taste the Rivel's were ready to serve. They were that simple and the creamy rich broth that they swam in was delicious. Everyone in our house enjoyed Rivel's except for father who complained they were too much like eating uncooked dough and did not care for them.

The homey aroma of the Rivel's filled the kitchen and I could hardly wait to wolf down a big'ol bowl of the creamy little darlings. With Aunt Ruby being our special guest she was served first and then me. The warm buttery milk and dumplings soothed my sore throat as they went down. Unfortunately for me, my eyes were bigger than my stomach that was by then the size of a pea. As much as I hated to stop eating I had too, I was stuffed but because I'd been ill, no one wanted to finish what I had left and so mother covered my bowl with a plate and assured me they would keep till later.

The few bites that I did eat was just enough to bolster me which was good because after our meal mother announced that she and her sister would be heading to the bingo parlor for a few hours and I was to be left in charge until father came home. I'd had about enough excitement for one day and so when they left I turned on the radio at a low volume and relaxed on the sofa while Evelyn and James amused themselves playing. The Atwater Kent Hour was midway through when Evelyn and James started nodding off and I told them to go to bed but they ignored my instruction and my head was too sore to argue so I let them fall asleep on the rug. The Happiness Boy's program was just starting when mom and Aunt Ruby returned from the bingo parlor boasting that, "out of town Ruby," had won one of the pots. They were in a really good mood but mom's mood soured when she realized that father was not yet home which made me feel sick again, not from the measles, but because I knew there would be a fight that night.

Mother and Ruby woke James and Evelyn up who were sprawled out on the floor and guided them to their room so they wouldn't walk into a wall being half asleep. After giving me permission to sleep with them instead of on the cot I gladly got up and crawled into bed with them. As usual our bedroom door was left ajar but because mother had turned up the volume on the radio I couldn't hear what they were saying. The only sound seeping through was that of the radio. The Capital theatre was playing and it was a good show but mother preferred the singing of The Happiness Boy's which had aired earlier in the evening.

It had been a long day and I must have fallen asleep quickly only to be awoken by mother screaming at dad for coming home so late which I found embarrassing. Aunt Ruby did her best to calm the situation but to no avail. Mother's fury would not be squelched as she was in the middle of a true dad bashing tirade and flew at him like a wild banshee.

All the commotion woke James and Evelyn too and together we huddled in the bed and prayed for the battle to end. It seemed like forever but eventually the screaming stopped and everything calmed down and we were able to go back to sleep only to be awakened again when mom came into our room and booted me back to the poxie-cot so she could sleep with Evelyn and James. She must have still been really upset with dad because all night long she beat the mattress with her foot and the sound of her repetitive thump, thump, thumping that I was so familiar with lulled me back to sleep.

When I got up the next day I found out that Aunt Ruby had bedded down on the sofa and was already up and in the kitchen cleaning up the aftermath from our parent's fighting. She'd set out some bowls and spoons on the table and pulled out a box of cereal from our pantry. Otto's Dairy had already made our morning delivery of two quarts of fresh milk which was good because mom had used the last of what we had preparing her Rivel's the night before. We were slurping down our corn flakes while Aunt Ruby started percolating a pot of coffee. She alerted us that there was a young man peeking in through our side door screen. Glancing over I saw that it was my friend Jeff standing there with his hands cupped around his face peering in. Because of him having the measles too it was his first day out of his house and had come over to see if I could come out and play. As soon as my aunt ascertained that the boy was a friend of mine she informed him that I was not yet ready to receive guest and sent him home. Before Jeff left I leaned over and gave him a wave letting him know I was still in the land of the living even though I might not have looked like it.

When we finished our cereal Aunt Ruby made comment that it was very thoughtful for Jeff to come around and hinted that he must be really smitten with me, to which I shrugged my shoulders not knowing. While the coffee brewed on the stove she went into the bathroom and began drawing me a much needed bath. After breakfast she gave Evelyn and James permission to play outside while I had a good long soak in the tub. It felt so good to wash off the grime from my body and out of my hair and I stayed in the tub for as long as the hot water allowed. After my bath Aunt Ruby invited me to sit down on the floor in front of the sofa near where'd she'd slept. The pillow and blanket was folded neatly and place on the edge of the couch. Painstakingly my aunt combed out a week's worth of tangles from my hair. It took her awhile but it gave us a chance to talk which was nice. It was great and I was appreciative of her help. I'd imagined if mother was to brush out my hair there would have been hell to pay knowing she'd have ripped through those tangles pulling my hair out by the roots like they weren't attached to my scalp and then for good measure she might have clobbered me upside my head with the brush before threatening to shave my head out of frustration.

After a good scrub down and comb-out I looked somewhat presentable and felt a world better too. We heard mother stirring in the other room. When she came into where we were mom looked as though she'd been through the mill too. Because I was sorted out and they wanted some privacy I was given permission to get dressed on go outside. As luck would have it Jeff was still around and riding his bike waiting for me. Both he and I were glad to be together again and after comparing notes about how sick the two of us had been Jeff asked who the lady was at our house. I explained that she was a visiting aunt from Indiana.

It was then that Jeff pulled something out of his pocket that he had wrapped in a handkerchief and handed it to me.

"For me," I asked coyly thinking my aunt was right about Jeff being smitten with me.

"It's not for you Rose, it's for your dad," he answered matter-of-factly.

"My dad?" I asked wondering what it was about.

Now I knew my father had always been kind to Jeff as he was to everyone but I was surprised that he had a gift for him. Jeff explained that he had started working on it before he got sick and that while he was in bed laid-up with the measles he was able to finish it. While unfolding the handkerchief I saw that it was a crudely carved wooden hand gun that, as far as I was concerned, looked so authentic it could be operational or at the very least used as a club. Jeff said he'd put the final touches to it that morning before he'd come around. Jeff cleverly had incorporated a layer of black shoe polish to darken the wood and I knew my dad would love it being a woodworker himself and although I thought it looked great I had to ask about why he'd carved a gun?

Jeff stated with conviction that it was what the block of wood wanted to be. I had no idea what he meant by that but it was clear that my friend possessed some talent and I knew the kind gesture would impress my father. When I told Jeff about my parents fight the night before and that now would not be a good time to bring a gun into our house even if it wasn't real. Then I told him my father wasn't home anyhow and that he could give it to him as soon as my parents made up and were in a better mood. Jeff looked disappointed but kept his gift until the following Saturday afternoon which was when I gave him the all clear. My Aunt Ruby had left to go back to her husband the day before and my mom had gone into town taking Evelyn and James with her. The coast was clear and everything was calmed down. With the house quiet and our guest gone my father decided to relax on the sofa and fell asleep listening to the radio. Jeff's timing was perfect and I couldn't wait to see the look on my dad's face when Jeff presented him with the gift. Quietly we tiptoed in and stood next to the couch where my father laid napping.

The radio was softly playing in the background and although Jeff didn't want to disturb my father, I insisted that it would be alright. We weren't going to have a better opportunity and so I gently patted my father's leg whispering, "wake up daddy, daddy wake up."

When my father opened his eyes and saw the likes of us standing there bold as life he woke up swinging. To my father we looked like a couple of pint sized armed marauders with a gun stuck in his face. It all happened so fast Jeff and I jumped back to get out of the way of being punched in the face. During all the commotion I'd accidently knocked over one of mom's figurines but fortunately, it didn't break. Father's kneejerk reaction scared the wits out of us as apparently we'd done the same to him. He yelled at us for nearly giving him a heart attack and warned that under no uncertain terms were we ever to wake him like that again. As soon as he gained his composure, we all caught our breath as Jeff handed over the gift, grip first.

"What's this?" Dad asked taking it from Jeff's hand.

"It's for you."

"Why for how come?"

"Because, us Welsh stick together," Jeff stated which caused my father to chuckle and question who made it.

"I did." Jeff claimed.

"Ah come on, you did not." Dad said doubtfully.

"Did so!" Jeff defended.

Jeff might have sounded impertinent but father overlooked it because of the gift.

"Well I'll be darned," dad said looking the carving over.

"Well, well Rose, it seems your young man has some real talent but why a gun?" my father asked.

As Jeff shrugged his shoulders I interjected that the wood told him what it should be. My father, a woodworker himself, understood and said something about Jeff being a chip off the old block as he rustled his hair playfully.

Pleased with his gift, father commented on how perfectly proportioned the barrel was to the stock and said that such a fine piece deserved a proper display. Jeff had not thought of that but was very excited by the suggestion. Dad invited Jeff into his private woodshop in the backyard. Proudly, the three of us walked single-filed with my dad leading the way. Once inside the shed, dad pointed to some planks of wood that he kept stacked in the far corner near the wood stove and asked Jeff to pick one out. Jeff looked as though he was afraid to disturb the stack and wasn't sure what size would be needed for the job.

He held up a plank and asked, "Will this one do?"

The board Jeff chose was a little warped and so my dad discarded it and found a better piece to use. Jeff was aware of the woods imperfection but felt uncomfortable picking out a piece for the project.

Now my father had never thrown away a single scrap of wood no matter how small or warped it had become. If it was not fit for use it could always be burned in the woodstove to heat the shed when it got cold. Either way my father would not waste wood.

The mount was of a simple design. Dad penciled out the two pieces needed for the project and handed Jeff a pair of safety glasses to wear as he showed him how to use a band-saw safely. Jeff was eager to learn and dad helped guild the wood through the turns with caution. They only needed two pieces and after they were cut out dad handed Jeff a piece of extra fine sandpaper to smooth out the barrel prop. It resembled a lopsided slingshot. While Jeff worked on the one piece father worked on the other and rounded off the rough edges. They sanded both pieces smooth before affixing them together the barrel prop to the main base. Once assembled the mount was then stained walnut. Dad said they they'd done enough for the day and after setting the wood aside to dry sent Jeff home to eat. After our supper father excused himself and went back out to his woodshop alone. I didn't see him again until he came into our room and kissed our foreheads and sang us a song goodnight.

Jeff came by our house after church the following day anxious to see the gun mounted properly. When my dad saw Jeff coming up the walk he met him in the driveway before inviting him in. Sitting on the end table mysteriously draped with the handkerchief Jeff had initially wrapped the gun in sat the finished gun mount. It was very exciting.

"Ta da!" dad said as he lifted the handkerchief.

It was a fantastic surprise especially for Jeff who nearly fell over when he saw what my father had added to their project. The center of the base held an inset brass nameplate with the inscription, "Handcrafted by Jeff Davis" and it was dated. Neither of us could believe our eyes. Jeff had never seen his name displayed so boldly for all to see and so he ran his finger over the engraving before rubbing off his fingerprint smudge with his sleeve to buff the plate back up. He didn't want the oil and salt from his hands mar the brass. Jeff noticed that dad had left the bottom unstained so when my father was out of the room, Jeff set the gun aside and carefully flipped the mount over and while using a sharp pencil printed out my father's name in his best penmanship. It turned out to be a lovely piece of art which we proudly placed in a prominent area of our living-room out of everyone's reach, especially James who was always itching to get at it.

CHAPTER SEVEN
THE MISHAP

When my fathers' family first immigrated to America from Wales, dad was just a boy. Because they were Welsh, first and foremost; singing became a major part of their life. The Evan's family sang at the kitchen table, in the bath, at church, in the mines, before going to bed and at every outing we'd ever gone on. The constant voice training helped my father develop a beautiful pitch and a rich tenor's tone that resonated harmoniously with every note he sang. Everyone enjoyed listening to my father belt out a tune. Strangers and friends encouraged my father to get into vaudeville instead of the mines and millwork but father claimed that if a man don't work he can't eat and that he could never, in his wildest dreams, think of singing a song as work. For him it was sheer pleasure.

During those long summer months when the sun was high but just barely visible because of the factory smoke billowing from every chimney along the three rivers; the heat could be more oppressive than the choking smog surrounding our town. Whenever the air was even the least bit tolerable, mom would go about the house opening our windows wide enough to allow what little breeze there happened to be inside.

My favorite days were when I was out in the yard and could hear my father's melodic voice drifting softly through the air straight to my ear long before I could see his form walking up our road. My hearts excitement over my father coming home to spend time with us soared higher than if I'd discovered a buried treasure in the yard. I'd drop whatever I was doing and run straight towards his voice and hug his waist with great enthusiasm to greet him even before he stepped through the haze and into view.

Oftentimes we'd missed seeing our father during the day. Whatever time he came home no matter how late it was he would come into our room and serenaded us with a song before kissing our foreheads and wishing us pleasant dreams. Mom usually attempted interceding, on our behave, complaining that he was just a stupid drunk who, if he had any sense at all, should leave us alone and go to bed, but her pleas never worked. Dad would not rest until he saw our little faces snuggled serenely in our bed, and after staggering into our room, despite mom's insistence that he didn't come in, dad would kneel down like child getting ready to pray and softly sing us a lullaby sending us sailing smoothly back into the transitional dreamland from whence we had just come.

Mom was right, in that we were usually awoken by dad's arrival home, but it was more often than not, from her arguing with him that disturbed our slumber and not his singing to us. It always set my mind at ease knowing that my father had made it home safe and sound, from wherever he'd been that evening. Within a few minutes of listening to his calming voice and feeling his soothing presence in the room, all three of us would gently doze off as though we'd never been disturbed at all. He may have had booze on his breath but he always had a smile on his face and a song in his heart. Mother could only see his faults and readily pointed them out to him in front of family, friends, strangers and the like. All I saw was a wonderfully clever handsome man who loved us dearly and I was proud to have him as my father. The reoccurring abandonment, that I know bothered mom more than his drinking, was the only thing I ever faulted him for as a child but even I understood that a working man needed to unwind after a hard day at the factory. He was a good provider and in my eyes he could do no wrong. I loved him so.

Our father's family lived approximately sixty miles or so south of Pittsburgh in the small coalmining town of New Salem. Grandma Mari and Grandpa Rhodri, along with my Aunt Catherine, Uncle Morgan, Uncle Dai and Dai's wife Auntie Ann, all lived there. Auntie Ann's mother, Catherine Hennessey, was a neighbor of theirs and remained Grandma Mari's closest friend until her death during the winter blast of 1923. Dad's only sister, my Aunt Catherine, was named after Auntie Ann's mother. We rarely seen much of them, although I wish we could have gone there more often.

It was always such a treat to see and enjoy my father's old stomping ground, especially New Salem's baseball diamond atop a place we called Diamond Hill. Dad loved baseball and from what grandpa always told us about my father was that he was a natural athlete. Dad still played for the steelworks back home in Pittsburgh but because mom was not a fan of the sport she never bothered to take us to see him play although I would have loved to have gone to see my father in action.

It was mid June and after finally completing my third year in school I was out for the summer. Evelyn had completed two years and James would be attending school in the fall. Understanding the difficulty of arranging holidays around our school schedule father felt a family vacation to his folk's home was in order and so we packed a valise and headed south to New Salem.

It was early in the morning when we got on the road and already it was a miserably hot summer's day which would prove to be a real scorcher. Mom sat up front in the passenger seat with James while Evelyn and I were cooped up in the back and father of course was driving. The appreciated breeze streaming in through our cars open windows made sitting in the backseat with Evelyn almost bearable. Every time the road turned sharply Evelyn slid her hot sweaty body over to mine squishing me onto the door panel like it was some kind of a joke. She was really ticking me off and I kept shoving her back to her own side of the seat but she just would not quit. Mom glanced back a couple of times to see what was going on but her head could only turn so far and so every time she looked all she could see was me shoving Evelyn back to her own side of the car. When I shrugged my shoulders in quiet protest proclaiming my innocence and pointed at Evelyn to blame her, mom didn't see it that way and shook her finger at me as a warning to behave myself and I took her warning very serious.

Not wanting to get into trouble I came up with a plan for the next time Evelyn tried her antics. When the next bend in the road came and Evelyn slid over and I jumped over her lap as though we were playing leap frog and took over her side of the car. Once I was on the other side I held fast to my new position and made Evelyn stay on the driver's side of the car. The strategy worked to my advantage better than I'd imagined. My hope was that the next time mom turned her head she would be able to see who was actually causing the trouble and that for once, it wasn't me. The unpleasantness I was made to endure if and when I ever made Evelyn cry was something I would avoid at all cost. Whenever Evelyn turned on the waterworks, mother would start yelling at me; dad would then threaten to pull the car over where he would take his belt off and blister my behind. All I wanted to do was get to grandmas without incident and felt it was best I mind my P's and Q's.

My switching seats with Evelyn turned out to be a brilliant move, for me anyhow, not so much for Evelyn. Within twenty minutes of our impromptu seat change dad coughed up a great big slimy hocker and spat it out the car window as he drove. Evelyn leant the wrong way at the wrong time and caught the bulk of that nasty lugie straight in her face.

Evelyn's expression when dad's leggy green phlegm ball hit her in the chops was priceless, gross and for me hysterically funny all at the same time and I nearly wet my pants trying to hold back the laughter. No one else in the car seemed to appreciate the humor in what had happened besides me. Evelyn was quite literally "gob-smacked" and my finding it amusing didn't help matters.

Dad felt really badly about what he'd accidently done to his little girl and immediately pulled the car over and parked so Evelyn could get cleaned up before she threw up from the grossness of it all. While mom and dad took care of Evelyn's predicament I took advantage of the time off the road and relieved myself in the grass behind a stand of nearby trees. As soon as Evelyn and I were both sorted out we were made to switch places again when Evelyn refused to sit behind dad. After the whole flying-hocker episode no body blamed her but I knew dad would be more careful the next time he coughed something up and so gladly I took my place behind the driver's side of the car. It seemed that Evelyn had learned her lesson and stayed on her own side of the car for the rest of the trip refusing to even look in my direction which was good because I was having a hard time keeping my composure and did not want to get in trouble for laughing.

The instant our car pulled up in front of dads folk's house, everyone we cared about, was there to greet us. It was not yet noon but the oppressive sun was already beating down so hard I thought I would melt into a puddle on the ground and die. Dad, grandpa, Uncle Dai and Morgan stood out front under the shade of a tree enjoying a bottle of granddad's homemade beer while we and the ladies stepped inside the house to freshen up after our trip. Grandma confessed to mother that grandpa had concocted a fresh batch of beer in honor of our arrival but mother did not seem pleased by the news but for once, did not say anything about it. After rewashing Evelyn's face with some proper soap and water Auntie Ann stripped her drooling toddler named Thomas down to his diaper and mopped his face, arms and belly with a damp cloth to cool him down. It looked like a brilliant idea to me and so without thinking I asked permission to take my dress off and was pleasantly surprised when mother allowed me to do it. Happily I stripped down to my panties and ran outside to enjoy my newfound freedom but the instant my father got a load of me running around outside and unclothed he choked on his beer and spat out a mouthful of grandpa's homemade brew and demanded me back to the house and put my dress on. Stupidly I argued that mom said it was alright, which did not sit well with him. Dad apparently did not care who gave me the permission but he would have none of it and followed me to confront her about my indecent display.

Mom did not see what the big deal was but father stood his ground thinking otherwise. Their bickering over something I'd asked for made me feel bad. Before their heated discussion turned too ugly I went into the other room and tried my best to pull my damp wrinkled dress over my sweaty body which was no easy task. That darn dress came off a heck of a lot easier than it went back on and I could have used some help but was afraid to ask for any knowing I had already asked for too much. My struggle continued until I was able to pull it down over my waist and while still tugging at the seams and feeling sorry that I had asked to take off the stupid dress in the first place I raced into the kitchen before everyone was made uncomfortable by my parents tiff.

It was one of my first lessons in the social imbalance between little boys and girls and with their little spat over father announced that he needed to take a walk and I was thrilled when he offered to take me with him. Dad and I were not yet out the door before mom called us back insisting we take Evelyn too. Thankfully mom recognized that James would have been a something of a handful and was in need of a nap. Mom stretched her arms and yawned declaring she was worn out from the trip and needed to unwind which I thought that was funny because I was wound up tighter than a drum after being trapped in the backseat next to Evelyn all morning. Dad went into the cellar while mom and James headed up the stairs with the intention of putting James down for a nap.

When father came up from the basement he had his mitt, ball and bat I worked out where we were going and was very excited about it. As we walked I volunteered to shag the balls for dad in the hopes of making up for my earlier transgression about the dressing episode, to which his only response was, "we'll see."

The long and winding dusty path was grooved deeply from years of townie foot traffic trampling its ascending route. The scenery atop Diamond Hill was spectacular and second to none. Even when there were no games on the dockets, some of the locals took advantage of its scenic benefits. Father said that when he was young it was the place where prospective sweethearts met. The setting would have been perfect for a romantic picnic where they could woo their loved one in peace. Dad said that he'd brought mom up there when they were first married and that he would never forget the lovely time they shared atop Diamond Hill. It was hard for me to imagine mom actually once liked him but appreciated that it had happened and that they both had enjoyed the view an idyllic picnic and each other's company. If that breathtaking view of the purple hued Allegheny Mountain range nestled in the distant horizon could kindle their romance it had to be a truly magical place.

Where the path leading to the diamond started was where the rows of company housing, called the patch, ended. It was a pleasurable walk to New Salem's old baseball diamond, for the most part anyway. The downhill slope wound around the far end of the housing complex where it took a sharp dogleg left and up to Diamond Hill at the banks of an old stagnate pond that stunk to high heaven. That small pool of water always gave me the creeps as dad said it did him when he was a boy.

Rumor had it that it was full of quicksand and that a slimy bog monster would crawl out of its mire at night and roam the patch in search of fresh young children to eat. After a year of believing the folklore dad assured me that it was all made up which confused me because he was the one who told me the story in the first place and grandpa Evan's and both Uncle Dai and Morgan confirmed it to be true. Whether the story were real or not I could not help but imagine all kinds of horror stories about what lurked below its murky water. The children of New Salem would sometimes toss rubbish into the pond. Some of it sank and some of it did not which added to its creepiness. There was a muck covered one-eyed doll head floating alongside some probable chicken bones and the likes. The dolls detached body had drifted or was tossed on the other side of the pond and was hung up by its moss covered leg that was stuck in a slimy tireless spoke rim that had partially sunk into the muddy bank. I hated walking next that swamp but it was the only way we knew to get to our destination.

Diamond Hill was where my father's father taught him the game and it was therefore fitting that it would be where my father would teach me. Dad loved baseball and because James was still too young at the time, dad decided he would teach me the basics, despite the fact that I was a girl. I loved tossing the ball back and forth to him. Father claimed that like him, I too was a natural. He often held his mitt in different positions in order to teach me how to control my pitching. My aim was to hit his gloves pocket without dad having to move an inch. After I was good at tossing the ball to him dad decided it was time for me to learn how to bat a ball.

I'll never forget when I got my first hit. Dad and I had worked on my batting stance while Evelyn wandered around gathering wildflowers to take back to mom and grandma. Using a stick dad drew a box in the sand and positioned me in the rectangle. We had a makeshift home plate which consisted of a discarded license plate that we'd found near the bog during our walk up the hill to the diamond. With everything ready dad handed me the bat and placed my hands snuggly one on top the other with my right hand above my left. The bat was heavy and so I allowed it to rest on my shoulder while dad stepped back a few steps and got ready to pitch me the ball. Dad asked Evelyn if she would play catcher but warned her to keep back while I was swinging the bat. Dad stretched and wound up like he was going to pitch me a fast ball only to slow up and gently toss the ball in my direction, about chest high. He called out for me to swing and I obliged and swung awkwardly, hitting nothing but air. Evelyn excitedly did her part as catcher and ran to fetch the rolling ball before throwing it in dad's direction. Father commended Evelyn on what a good job she was doing and told me to ready myself for another try at batting.

"OK, Rose, this is it. Get ready, here it comes," he warned me before gently tossing the ball for the second time.

Again I swung, but I was having some trouble controlling the heavy wooden bat. Dad came over and showed me what he meant when he told me to choke up on the bat and shifted my hands higher up the shaft. His simple suggestion worked like a dream and suddenly the bat did not feel so heavy and I had more control. We persevered until I got my first real hit. Now that ball may not have gone very far, but my spirit soared well beyond the outfield. It was a magical moment and one that would not to be soon replicated. The elation on dads face when my bat connected with that ball was amazing.

Father's glee over the hit bolstered my confidence and I wholly believed that I was capable of hitting that darn ball out of the park and could not wait to show him my natural ability for batting. After letting the bat's halt rest on my shoulder I spat on my hands and rubbed them together. I was not sure why people did it but I'd seen my father do it a number of times before batting and so I thought it couldn't hurt. Dad bent slightly over and slapped the ball a couple of times into his mitt.

"Okay Rose you can do it," he said smiling broadly before tossing me the ball.

With all the strength I could muster I swung so hard that the bat slipped out of my sweaty little hands and shot off spinning through the air like a Whirling Dervish aimed straight at Evelyn's unsuspecting head. As soon as dad saw what was happening he threw down his mitt and raced towards Evelyn just as the hilt of the bat connected with her nose. She rolled around on the ground clutching her face screaming bloody murder which was terrifying and for a second I feared I'd killed her. Just like dad didn't mean to hit her with his hocker, I never meant to club her in the head with my bat and I felt terrible about it. After a quick assessment of the damage dad methodically pulled a handkerchief from out of his back pocket and applied pressure to Evelyn's nose while calmly reassuring her that she was going to be alright. Still, it was very scary and there was a great deal of blood all over her face, hands and dress.

Dad cleaned her up a little before lifting her and cradling her in his arms as if she were a newborn baby which calmed Evelyn's hysteria. Without saying a word to me, dad got up from the ground and left the field carrying Evelyn off the pitch and down the path towards grandma and grandpa's house where we would have to face mom and explain what had happened.

After already causing one argument that day it looked as though because of something else I'd done they'd be arguing all over again and I was not looking forward to it. With my stomach in knots I pondered what had just happened. Listlessly I began gathering the baseball equipment that dad had left behind. Because father was practically running I'd lost a lot of ground and even though I did my best to catch up to them there was no way I was going to.

Finding my way back to the house was not a problem but lugging all the equipment was turning out to be. While daydreaming and lost in thought I wandered down the hill only to find myself standing next to that scary swamp and this time I was without the benefit of my father's protection. The only weapon I had was my dad's bat and that was when it hit me that I would have to face my mom all by myself because dad and Evelyn were so far ahead of me. By the time I got back to grandma's, mother would have known what I'd done to Evelyn and the fear of her reaction superseded that of the stupid bog monster. Between the two of them, if they were to battle my bet would have to be on mom and halfheartedly I wished the bog monster were real so he could come and drag me into the swamp to put me out of my misery. No bog monster could be more frightening than the thought of facing my mom when she was riled up and because I was in no hurry to die I took my sweet time getting back to the house. Uncle Morgan had come looking for me and helped me carry the baseball equipment the rest of the way. When we got there everything had settled down and Evelyn was given a special treat for being so brave.

Our visit to New Salem ended up turning out well, at least as far as I was concerned. Firstly, Evelyn learned to stay on her own side of the car and I learned a little about the game of baseball from my father which was a fantastic memory. For me the highlight of our trip was the instant my bat connected with that ball and I got my first real hit. In all fair conscience I didn't count my second hit as a highlight because it was Evelyn's face that got creamed and not the face of the ball but it did teach me to hold on to the bat instead of throwing it. Just as Evelyn survived the batting incident and I too survived facing mom after the fact. As usual mother turned out to be more upset with father than she was with me because he'd not watched out for Evelyn better and so besides the arguments and Evelyn looking like a raccoon from her blackened eyes, I had a good time.

Later that same year Evelyn was able to exact her revenge on me. It was around Easter weekend and we were in our bed and mother in hers. Dad had already left for work hours earlier when the incident happened. For once James and I were fast asleep while Evelyn, for some inexplicable reason, was sitting up in bed fiddling with an umbrella. When I rolled over she opened the umbrella poking me in the corner of my eye with one of its metal spines that stick out around the outer edge. That umbrella got me good, perforating the inside corner of my right eyeball. It burned like the dickens and I shouted in pain but because mother was such a sound sleeper she had not heard me and so not wanting Evelyn to get away with what she'd done I went straight to her bedroom cupping my injured eye and stood next to her bed and woke her up. There seemed to be some moisture building up in my hand but I wasn't what it was.

When mom opened her eyes I removed my hand revealing my eye as a timely mixture of clear fluid streaked with blood rolled down my cheek and dripped off my chin creating a dramatic effect that made my mom scream out in horror.

"Look at what Evelyn did!" I cried out.

There was no more pain but when mom panicked I did too. The provability of me losing my eye in a stupid umbrella accident had not even crossed my thoughts but the way my mother was carrying on I feared it might be a possibility. That was when the images of that ugly one eyed dolls head I'd seen floating around in New Salem's swampy bog came to mind.

"Was this my fate to run around with only one eye?"

At the time my only conciliation was the knowledge that Evelyn was going to get into big trouble this time and rightly so. What the heck was she thinking bringing an umbrella into our bed?

Everything turned out alright though. Evelyn got her butt whipped for what she'd done to me and mom healed my eye with a dab of ointment and a piece of gauze. Fortunately I suffered no vision loss and my eye healed quickly. From then on Evelyn was band from operating an umbrella while in the house.

CHAPTER EIGHT
CELESTIAL POWERS THAT BE

In mid October my dad felt that another family trip to New Salem was in order. We were very excited but at the time both Evelyn and I were attending school and so we could only go for a short weekend getaway. The reason for the trip was that our grandfather was about to turn sixty and grandma had planned on throwing him a celebratory party that she wanted us to attend. In the beginning it was an uneventful trip, until for some reason I came up with the bright idea of dangling a pair of James bib overalls out the car window to amuse myself and watched as they flapped in the breeze. My grip turned out to be stronger than the fabric and the trousers went sailing down the road and I was left holding the strap. I knew I was in for it even though Evelyn was sleeping at the time and had not seen what I'd done or she would have told on me for sure. I found it hard to tell on myself but knew I had to do it and the sooner the better, the longer I waited the worse it would be for me so putting my fears aside I passed the torn strap up to the front over mother's shoulder.

"What's this?" mother asked before screaming for dad to stop the car.

"Will you never learn!" she yelled jumping out of our car while it was still rolling having not come to a complete stop.

Father didn't know what was going on or why mother was running down the road but he too got out of the car and went to help mom. Our abrupt stop caused Evelyn to wake and ask me, if we were there yet?

After a quick search mom and dad returned to the car empty handed. They both looked pretty disgusted with me and for a second I thought dad was going to undo his belt which made my butt cheeks tighten. I was spared a licking but not a good bawling out for acting so stupidly and loosing James' pants. For me, it had proved to be a long and miserable trip and I was glad when we arrived at grandma and grandpa's house for the party. As we pulled up in front of their house I was short of some dignity and James was short of a change of clothes.

Father insisted mother let the pants episode drop claiming he'd heard enough about it as I thought to myself "You think you've heard enough!"

Thankfully mother took dad's advice and let the subject drop and began fussing with her hair for a moment before getting out of the car. I'd never been so relieved to get somewhere in all my life. We all went inside and while the women began baking the celebratory cake for granddad we utilized mom's latest bit of advice which was for me to take a suggested hike.

Me, Grandpa, father, Uncle Dai, Evelyn and James all left while the women stayed behind baking. Uncle Morgan was at work but was planning to join us later on for the party. There was a wooded glen across the way where father and Uncle Dai used to play when they were boys. When we got there they began pointing out where they'd dug out a fort in the earth some years earlier. The area was overgrown and a good deal of brush covered most of it but the hole was still there. At the site laid some of the original materials strewn about and after locating a downed tree for us to sit on with granddad, dad and uncle Dai went to work reconstructing their makeshift fort. It was good fun to watch them acting like kids again and you could tell they too were having fun. When they finished it looked so small I didn't know how they and their friends ever fit inside but with their mission completed dad and Uncle Dai surprised us by opening a couple of tins of beans in tomato sauce that they had been toting. A pocket knife was used to open the cans but they warned that the edges were jagged and could cut us if we weren't very careful. After passing out some spoons we all dug in.

It was the first time I'd eaten cold beans straight out of the tin but had to admit they tasted pretty darn good. After the trauma I'd suffered by losing James' pants, our time in New Salem was quickly turning into another wonderful memory that I would never forget and for me, the best was yet to come. While we ate the beans granddad rehearsed some tales of yore from when they were growing up in Wales. Now my father and Uncle Dai must have heard those stories at least a dozen times before but they still sat respectful and listened as though it was their first time to hear them. It had been a long day and by the time we got back to the house James was worn out and practically falling asleep although he would never admitted defeat.

A heavenly aroma was coming from the kitchen and while the cake cooled mother took James upstairs and made him lay down so he could take a nap. As soon as he fell asleep she came back down with his dirty pants in her hand. Because James no longer had a change of clothes and his pants were soiled from our day trip to the woods mother had stripped them off him and washed them and hung them out to dry. Having no desire to be reamed out a second time for losing the trousers I thought it wise to stay clear and played quietly in the front yard.

By the time James woke from his slumber our supper was ready and the cake was frosted and waiting for us to enjoy. The beans we ate earlier had worn off and we were all hungry again. The food smelt good but Granddad's birthday cake was what I was looking forward to and it was good. After the women cleared the table and all the dishes were dried and put away the adults prepared to partake in a lively game of pinochle which was at the time grandpa's favorite card game and because it was his birthday he got to choose what game they would play.

While the adults set up their game Evelyn, James and I went outside to play tag and Red Rover with a few of the neighborhood kids that we'd become acquainted with over the years. Normally we were called in as soon as it got dark but because it was a special occasion and our folks were having a good time we were allowed to continue playing outside later than usual. It felt exhilarating and a little naughty to be outside after dusk unsupervised. We all started to scream when a squadron of local bats came out of their caves and swooped and darted around us. It was a little scary and so we covered our heads and ran to the porch and stood under the roof for protection. Granddad had said in one of his stories that when a bat flies to close it could get stuck in your hair where it would lay its eggs and drive you crazy. It sounded awful and so we made sure our heads were covered. James thought they were funny to watch for awhile but he soon grew bored with it and went inside to join the adults. Evelyn stayed out with me even after the neighbor kids went home for the night.

October's harvest moon was magnificent that night and we watched as it rose heavily and loomed above the hilly horizon looking like a great orangey ball sporting a somber gray face complete with two eyes and nose and mouth. It appeared to be so close you would think you could reach out and touch it. It was a mystifying moment, at least for me.

Like James, Evelyn soon became bored and wanted to go inside but I asked her to stay awhile longer and she did. For once, Evelyn was being a good sport but soon fell asleep leaning on my shoulder. Because we lived in Pittsburgh and there was so much factory smoke in the air and we weren't allowed out after dark we'd never seen much of the evening sky.

It did not take long before father came out onto the porch to stretch his legs and to check on us. When he saw that Evelyn had already fallen asleep he thought it best that I come inside too.

"Ah, dad, do I have to?" I asked, pleading to stay a bit longer.

"Rose, what do you want to stay out here for?" he asked.

"Look at the moon, daddy."

"Yeah she's a beauty, alright." He said picking Evelyn up to carry her inside.

"Can I stay just a little bit longer?"

"Oh I suppose, but don't you leave the porch."

"Thank you, daddy, I promise."

While mother rarely denied Evelyn the things she asked for father rarely denied me. After he had carried Evelyn inside to put her to bed he brought me out a blanket and laid it over my shoulders. I had not felt the cold until he covered me with the blanket and had to admit it did feel good and warm. Because the adults were taking a little break dad came back out and sat with me and began pointing out some of the more notable stars and constellations. The big dipper turned out to be one of my favorites, simply because it was the first constellation I could make sense of. When granddad called for father to come back to their card game he again allowed me to stay on my own. The stars and planets made me to wonder if my friends back in Pittsburgh had ever seen such a site. It seemed such a shame that our smoggy skies concealed so much wonderment that none of us knew was there and I could not wait to share my experience with Jeff.

The next person to come out the door and check on me was my grandmother Evans. She sounded concerned and asked if I were alright to which I answered that I was fine. Grandma could see that I was safe and warm and was not causing any harm and so she went back to their card game where I overheard her take my defense stating that I wasn't hurting anything. I could hear father state from the table, "Ah, let her be. Come on mom, it's your deal."

That was when I heard my mother comment that I never knew when to quit. Granddad and grandma corrected her by stating that they thought I was lovely, which made me feel good and smile. It was a magical night and as the sky darkened to a rich navy blue more and more stars became visible. There were some distant crickets chirping happily from a neighbor's yard as I sat on the porch wrapped tight in my blanket. The muddled banter of the adult's laughter seeped outside from the kitchen through the screen door. They seemed to be having a good time smoking their cigarettes and playing their friendly game of cards. Evelyn and James were already fast asleep and I was alone appreciating the view. All was right with the world when a brilliant streak of sparkling light shot across the sky only to fade away before my very eyes like it had never happened. The spectacle made me to run inside excitedly telling everyone what I'd just seen thinking it had never happened before. Granddad explained that it was called a shooting star which described what I'd just seen perfectly. Grandpa also said that they were lucky and that the next time I saw one I should make a wish.

"Will it come true?" I asked excitedly.

"Of course, a shooting star wish is powerful stuff. They always come true," granddad assured me, and father concurred.

They explained that the next time I saw one I was to shut my eyes and make my wish. When I heard their story I was disappointed that I didn't know the power of the stars earlier. Excited by my newfound wisdom and after gaining permission to go back out to look for another it did not take long before I saw another even more magnificent than the first. Cautiously I held my breath, closed my eyes and made my wish. The wish was to see a hundred more and to my amazement the heavens opened and shooting stars begun zigging and zagging all across the velvety blue sky. It was awesome and I realized granddad was right about shooting stars being powerful and that their wishes really do come true. The astrological spectacle in front of me continued on for what must have been an hour. My oohing and aahing stopped as abruptly as our car did earlier that day and a feeling of dread rushed over me.

"What in the world had I done?" I thought to myself, worried that my thoughtless wish might have caused every star in the sky to burn up made me sad.

The fear that no one would ever again be able to admire their beauty would all be my fault. How could I deprive my own father and grandfather of something they had found so comforting?

Dad was familiar with many of the constellations, some he learned as a boy and some others he learned while overseas and in the Army. Father told me when he and his family first moved to America that the planet and stars was his first signs of normalcy. Once I realized I had the power over the stars and what I'd done, I quickly made my second wish for them to stop shooting before it was too late and they all burned up. Without waiting around I went back inside feeling confident that I'd made my second wish in the nick of time. As soon as I went inside I was tired and ready for bed. Having just saved the universe, plum wore me out but magic of that night would impact me for the rest of my life. The card game was still going strong when I came inside and although I'd gone to bed and was sleepy, sleep eluded me and I was having trouble getting off. My thoughts kept drifting beyond the stars and all galaxies until finally I must have fallen asleep because I dreamed pleasantly throughout the night.

Early the next morning we were awoken and got ready to attend church. It was a short walk into town and when we entered God's house James sat with the adults while Evelyn and I was sent to Sunday school. Our Sunday bible school lesson was on the story of David and Goliath and how a young boy slew a great giant with only a sling and a stone. When our Sunday school teacher talked about the one stone shooting across the valley before it stuck fast into Goliath's forehead killing him where he stood I couldn't help thinking about all those shooting stars I'd seen the night before.

When church was over and we were on our way back to grandma's and granddad's the sky turned a nasty shade of greenish gray just as the winds picked up and started blowing something fierce. As we stepped into the house the heavens opened up and it began to rain and not just your average downpour but a real toad strangler, as grandpa called it. Dad wasn't fussed about the delay of getting on the road because he had no intentions of driving home in the middle of a terrible storm even though he needed to work the next morning. We knew he would make it to work even if he needed to drive through the night. When a big clap of thunder sounded it shook the house and we all practically jump out of our skin.

There was no doubt that the lightning bolt had hit very close. To take our minds off the frightening storm raging outside granddad used its opportunity for a teaching moment. He informed us that to determine how close the lightning had struck we could countdown from the time we saw the lightning bolt to when we heard the clap of thunder and according to granddad's own calculations the last one that struck was practically atop of us.

Because the house had grown so dark grandma fetched the kerosene lamp from the other room and lit it. Between the flickering lamp light and the rain pounding the roof it was the perfect setting for more storytelling from our granddad.

"Back in the day…." was how grandpa normally started his tales and this one would be no exception.

For him reminiscing about his old schooldays was his favorite subject and it made me wonder why the old folks would go on so much about how tough they had it growing up and that the children of my generation would never be able to, "Cut the mustard," as it were. That old adage, in particular, always grossed me out. The mere visualization of that pasty yellow goo thickening into a brown inedible cracked gob of cement that had to be hacked at with a knife flipped my stomach every time. To my way of thinking, it was not that we could not cut the mustard; I didn't understand why anyone would want to try to.

We as children had already learned that we were never to act up in the company of adults, especially in front of my dad's mom and dad, and although this time seemed more relaxed because of the storm I purposely stayed on my best behavior and so did Evelyn and James.

It seemed more than coincidental that both my parents and their parents spun of the same yarns of woe concerning their upbringing and their attending of school and I could almost hear the violins' playing softly in the background every time they talked of their ordeals and endless walking of miles and miles up hill in the middle of great snowstorms and through spring thaws or rockslides only to attend a poorly constructed schoolhouse that had no amenities' like the fancy one-roomed school we attended in Pittsburgh. By their accounts if what they claimed were true all their schools were cave dwellings carved out of a mountain in a mythical place far, far away because it seemed that no matter what direction they were traveling they were always heading up hill and in foul weather.

If there had been a contest about the best, worst, school story ever, Grandpa Evans' would have won the prize hands down. As the rain hammered down outside and we huddled around the lamps flickering light Grandpa began his tale of young Thaddeus Vick. Like grandpa, Thaddeus grew up in Wale's where the two of them attended primary school. When the time came for testing both granddad and Thaddeus had scored extremely high scholastically and were then transferred to an advanced secondary school. Granddad described that particular school as a large brick and mortar structure styled in the grand Tudor design. The school was a Haberdashery run by a cruel Headmaster nicknamed "Head-Bastard Fearsome." Granddad called him that because his name was Pearson and we all chuckled when he said it. Even grandma grimaced ever so slightly when Grandpa said the B word.

Granddad had gone into great detail of how the headmaster looked and how he behaved. From his bowing back and baldy head to his deep furrowed brow and big sticky out ears that he claimed had enough hair growing out of them it appeared he were wearing earmuffs in the summertime. According to granddad Headmaster Pearson had bent legs, bad teeth, bad breath and a disgusting habit of pulling at his eyelashes only to eat them while sitting behind his desk. The very thought of him doing that made me gag and so it was no surprise that Grandpa labeled him as the ugliest man ever and that he was not only ugly on the outside he was nasty and depraved inside as well. Granddad said he roamed the school impatiently slapping a pointy long hardwood stick into the palm of his hand as he nervously awaited the chance to use his implement of torture on one of, "His Boys," and apparently Thaddeus had turned out to be one of those boys the Headmaster loved tormenting.

Thaddeus was described as a tall, fair-minded, soft-spoken bloke absent of malice. The new school they were to attend demanded a proper uniform which consisted of a green school crested blazer, white shirt a green and gold striped tie and black slacks which may not have been an issue for most families but it was for the Vick's and Thaddeus knew it. For that very reason, when it came time to take the scholastic test Thaddeus had even attempted to fail the exam so he would not have to switch schools but he was promoted nonetheless.

According to Granddad, Mr. Vick, Thaddeus's father had died some years earlier in a coalmine accident which left the Vick family destitute. The uniform issue created a real financial predicament and was a great hardship for the Vick's. Lacking the resources they put their heads together to see what they could come up with for Thaddeus. After rummaging around some old trunks his mother put her hands on an old military coat from some ancient conflict that they had tucked away in the chest. She might have been a novice seamstresses but she was glad for the opportunity to make it work. Painstakingly, she removed any and all military insignias, mended the moth holes. After shortening the sleeves and the jackets length she carefully re-stitched its silky green lining.

The blazer project took hours to complete but when she was finished was so pleased with her alterations that she partook in a jigger of port to celebrate the success. The off-colored blazer fit Thaddeus as though it had been professionally tailored by one of the royal seamstresses outfitting the queen. Proud of her accomplishment the next morning she sent Thaddeus to school and held her head high. Thaddeus had not been in the school long but already knew Head-Bastard Fearsome was not going to be pleased with his mother's effort but because she was so proud and had worked so hard on reworking that blazer he did not have the heart to disappoint her and wore it to school risking the criticism.

When Thaddeus arrived at school he purposely stood in the back row during their general assembly but because Thaddeus was taller than most of the other boy's Headmaster Pearson spotted him right away and summoned Thaddeus to the front of the class. With the entire student body assembled before him the Headmaster proceeded to humiliate poor Thaddeus unmercifully in everyone's presence. He made the joke that Thaddeus not only looked ridiculous but that he looked like a Japanese General. His cruel comment made everyone laugh except for Thaddeus. After the belittlement ended the flogging began and Thaddeus was beaten with a rod in front of a cringing student body and staff. The bright spot of grandpa's story was when Thaddeus ran into his nemesis, Headmaster Pearson, at a market place long after he'd retired and when he was no longer affiliated with the school. Mr. Pearson, it seemed, had all but forgotten about the Japanese General crack until Thaddeus reminded him of it and punched him in his nose as a reminder which was extremely gratifying for Thaddeus who'd never forget that humiliating day.

It was a very entertaining story and by the time granddad had finished it the rain had ended and we were ready to hit the road. It always struck me odd that no matter how awful a story was about the days of old I could always detect a certain glint of pride in the eyes of the storyteller. It looked as though those tough old times were the best days of their lives and that secretly they yearned for a chance to go back and relive them again.

Between my parents and grandparents I sometimes did not know what I should believe. I never wanted to think that they would deliberately lie to us about anything, but there was that Santa Clause, Easter Bunny, Tooth-fairy and bog monster episode and the moment I questioned my parents about their existence, I was pulled into the conspiracy so quickly my head spun as they made me swear an immediate allegiance so Evelyn and James would not discover the truth.

Grandpa Evan's stories may have seemed bigger than life, but so was he. The story of Thaddeus and Headmaster Fearsome was the last story I remember him telling us. I fell asleep on the drive back to Pittsburgh and dreamt about telling Jeff all the details of my magical night and my newfound powers over the stars. Jeff was eager to hear all about everything too and like usual walked me home after school. We chatted as we crossed the intersection past the snarled traffic in front of the Penn Street market after I had purchased a nickels worth of penny candies to share with Jeff.

Excitedly and while we sucked on our treats I described in great detail the wonderment of the heavens and Jeff believed me without question just like I knew he would. That was what I loved about Jeff Davis, no matter how incredible my story would have sounded to anyone else, Jeff trusted me with all his heart knowing that I would never lie to him, embellish maybe, but lie, never.

CHAPTER NINE
PITTSBURGH

A surge of reconstruction following WWI changed our city's skyline forever as massive buildings were being erected all over our expanding downtown. Father's job down at the mill was secure and he often worked sixty hour weeks and so because of it, between the mill and the bars, we did not get to see much of him.

The police and racketeers were fed up with the rhetoric of the prohibition laws and so they created an alliance. Bootleggers received the protection they desired and the speakeasies and stills were allowed to operate as usual. The participating police received free drinks as well as a flat fee to look the other way. Prohibition may have been enforced in Chicago and other parts of the country but here in Pittsburgh depriving a man from drink was considered criminal and so Pittsburgh was dubbed the wettest city in America and had the dubious reputation of being so wet you needed rubber boots to walk our streets.

During the industrial boom hordes of hungry able-body men from far and wide came to Pittsburgh in search of work. Ethnic communities popped up everywhere. We had Germans,

Syrians, Italians, Welsh, Hungarians, Irish, Finnish, Swedes and more. Mega companies like Westinghouse owned and operated multiple factories and employed thousands simultaneously. Westinghouse ran a machine plant, air brake factory, and of course there was Westinghouse Electric. All three companies were located in the down town area.

Entrepreneurs from all over gravitated to Pittsburgh because of the three rivers that converged on the city. Men like Henry Clay Frick, who, at a very young age, discovered himself to be a superb business organizer, and a genius in management. Henry began by keeping the books for his grandfather's distillery before operating some coke ovens in the surrounding coal district. He, not only saw the opportunity, he took the bull by the horns, as it were and purchased all the nearby coal lands for a mere pittance, during the panic of 1873. Subsequently Henry opened the H.C. Frick Coke Company and took his place amongst millionaire's row. Henry's servants tended his palatial estate that he affectionately named "Clayton." It was a sprawling, four story mansion complete with copulas, witches caped rooms and a massive covered front porch overlooking his immaculately manicured yard.

Fellow Welshman, Thomas Evans, unfortunately no known relationship to my father, Geraint Evans, owned Crescent Glassworks. Pittsburgh had Henry John Heinz, founder of the food-packing industry. Mr. Thomas Mellon established a private banking house on Smithfield Street which became T. Mellon & Sons and loaned money to fellow entrepreneurs coming onto the scene such as Andrew Carnegie, Captain "Bill" Jones, and Charles M. Schwab, to name only a few.

Construction was going on everywhere snarling traffic and making it tough to get around which was why my dad often road the cable car back and forth to the mill instead of driving his car. The newly completed Mellon Bank took up an entire city block and was years in the building. Erection of The Hotel Webster Hall and men's club and the new Chamber of

Commerce building made the magnificent Syria Temple look like small potatoes.

Pittsburgher's loved their sport and my father was no exception. Instilled within him was a deep appreciation for an athlete's ability and dad supported them with fervor. Whether they played for the Steelers, the Pirates or put their dukes up and boxed in the ring, dad followed them all.

One of father's favorite athletes was a local boy named Harry Greb, dubbed, "The Pittsburgh Windmill." Harry Greb was a boxer that had after a few fights acquired the reputation as a dirty fighter who could and would resort to whatever tactic it took to win his bout. Dad and his work buddies followed the young contender through every title fight he fought. Anticipation mounted when the news released that there would be a matchup between Harry and New York's Gene Tunney and that it was the American light heavyweight belt on the line. Their bout was to be held at a heaving Madison Square Garden and refereed by Kid McPartland. All those that could not attend the sold out match huddled around their radios so they could listen to blow by blow commentary. After the fight proud well wishers flooded the streets to see their Harry Greb return to Pittsburgh holding the title belt.

It was a glorious day for all Pittsburgher's until a year later Tunney regained the championship and Harry returned to the middleweight division where he won the world title. A year later he lost his title and while undergoing a simple eye surgery, died in hospital.

Another memorable time in Pittsburgh was when the Pirates played in the World Series. They had already won the prestigious title once and were vying for the trophy a second time. This series happened to be between Pittsburgh and the Washington Senators. The day prior to the Pirates playing a home game there was an accident at the mill. One of the men injured was laid up in the hospital and would be there for awhile. He held three prized tickets to the series and so when my father went to visit him in the hospital he reluctantly turned them over to my dad who gladly accepted them. They both knew it would be such a shame to let them go to waste and so when my dad came home that day holding the "Holy Grail," of tickets in his hand while excitedly announcing that Jeff and I were going to get to see "The World Series." We were beyond elated! Neither of us had ever stepped foot inside Forbes Field before and with this being the World Series the very thought of attending the game went beyond our wildest dreams.

It was a proud day walking into that grand stadium with my two favorite people in the whole world, Jeff and my dad. I guess it could have been better if our Pirates would have won that day but to top the thrill we were experiencing would have been hard to beat. We followed the away games on our radio and the home games outside Forbes Field with the rest of our gang. The Washington Senators went into the fifth game with a 3 to 1 lead. In an unheard of upset the Pittsburgh Pirates came back to win the next three games in a row. Game number seven was at home. Pittsburgh was heaving with excitement, ready to burst at the seams. And although it had started to rain by the ninth inning our spirits could not be dampened.

With 42,856 fans inside Forbes Field the rest of Pittsburgh united in their enthusiasm sending up a roar from the crowd that could be heard throughout the cities 28 wards when the Pirates own, Kiki Cuyler, hit a double bagger securing the four out of seven game victories. The final score was Pittsburgh Pirates 9 Washington Senators 7. The snarled traffic came to a grinding halt an all the downtown shopkeepers locked their doors after turning the closed signs towards the street so they too could join in the grand celebration that would go on well into the night. It was exciting and everyone that was a true baseball fan rallied in the moment.

CHAPTER TEN
DOILIES AND DILLIES

My father, I am proud to say, was one of those guys everyone enjoyed save one, his wife and my mother. On those rare occasions, when she wasn't furious with him, even she would have to admit she liked his company. Dad had sparkly blue eyes that lit up every time he regaled his eager audience with his spontaneous wit and observations. All of his stories were enchantingly classic and sure to please. They were as clever and colorful as his character itself. Not many people could render a more apt quip or could deliver it with such perfect timing as my father. He was one of a kind and wherever he was, inevitably, riotous laughter followed. Dad was the consummate entertainer in more ways than one.

Whenever my parents got together with their peers, one of two things happened. All the children would be excused from the room so they could have a good chinwag without worrying about some young tike hearing something inappropriate or on the rare occasions we were invited to stay as long as we could sit quietly and were respectful of our conduct.

Typically, for our family, Saturday evening was game night. That was when neighboring adults got together to unwind from the week and my folks were no exception. Mom and dad enjoyed entertaining and to be entertained. They had a handful of friends living nearby and so for them it was easy to meet up in the evening at one house or another for libations and amusement. Whenever they got together a cloud of smoke would fill the air thicker than the factory smoke billowing from every industrial downtown chimney.

While we never noticed it when it was happening the next day our clothes, hair and pores reeked with the sickly smell of cigarette smoke. It was a kind of traveling show where basically they just had fun. Sometimes they played dominoes and sometimes they would play a variety of card games depending on whose house they were in. One week the game would be at our house and the next week it would take place at a neighbor's house. Evelyn, James and I also had a gang of friends that we hung around with when our folks got together.

On one particular Saturday evening, while it was still light out, our parents were playing euchre at our house and we were in the front yard playing tag. While in the middle of our game Marcy tripped Susie which sent her flying through the air. When she landed she'd scrapped her knee badly on the pavement and so our game was suspended until she could have her wound tended too. Because we had an injured player down, our gang agreed we should suspend play until Susie's return. We needed a recess about then and I needed to use the bathroom. As I came rushing through the side door Evelyn made a decisive move and came through the front door beating me by a nanosecond to the toilet. While doing a pee-pee dance in the hall and banging on the door for her to hurry up one of my parent's guests, Miss Viola, a lady I liked, saw me waiting to use the bathroom and playfully stuck her tongue out at me but I stayed focused and in emergency mode and rushed in the second Evelyn turned the knob.

Miss Viola had an on again off again boyfriend named Lenny and the pair of them were a lot of fun to be around. Miss. Viola was a tall, thin, attractive woman that touted long dark wavy hair and whose distinct laugh sounded like a chicken getting ready to lay an egg. Her laughter always made me laugh. Her male friend Lenny worked down at the plant with my father. Mom and dad always teased that they should stop messing around and get married so they could be as happy as my parents were which always got a good laugh. They had dated for years but with no apparent plans of taking that next big step.

As I cut through the kitchen to rejoin my friends, Miss. Viola for a second time teasingly stuck her tongue out at me and without thinking I responded in kind and stuck my tongue out at her. It was all meant in fun but before I could recoil my tongue my father reached out across the table and busted me in the chops so fast my head spun. His knee-jerk slap made Miss. Viola feel horrible about what she had started and she instantly admitted her blame in the matter. She confessed that she was the instigator and not me and said that he was wrong for slapping me but my father would hear none of it. He then informed her that I'd been raised to know better than to disrespect an adult in that manner and that if she had a mind to ever do it again he would be obliged to slap her too.

Miss. Viola graciously accepted my father's explanation and shrugged at me apologetically promising she would never do it again. When I went back outside to play I still had dad's hand imprint and finger welts on my cheek. It was still stinging a bit but when I looked at poor Susie's bloody knee my pain went away and we resumed our game of tag.

I'd learned another valuable lesson that day; "Rules did not apply to Grownup's, only to us kids!"

My folks, for example, drank alcohol to excess, despite the laws of prohibition, indulged in smoking and cursing which intensified greatly whenever they were with their peers and especially while playing games. They could come and go as they pleased and for dad if he chose to stay out, he did. If we, as children, did any of those things we would have been switched for sure.

There was a different occasion when I slipped up and allowed a curse word to pass by my lips in front of my father. To say I had heard my father say that particular four letter word over a hundred times before was no exaggeration. Still, I was very much aware that I was never to utter it myself but accidents can happen but apparently not according to my dad. That tiny single syllable offense had barely sounded when I felt the pain of father's wrath on my face cheek and then carried over onto my butt cheeks shortly thereafter when he took off his belt. There was no getting around the fact that I had that one coming and I was thankful that I did not swear in front of mother instead. With mother, punishments had repercussions that could linger around for days, weeks, month's or in some cases years. Her form of discipline reminded me of someone cutting a pup's tail off an inch at a time with each chop hurting as bad as the first. Father's punishment's was always quick and fitted the crime.

Within our kitchen we kept an icebox. Our milk came courtesy of Otto's Dairy Farm and was freshly delivered every other day. Ice for the icebox came courtesy of Mr. Lazlo, the scariest man alive. Mr. Lazlo was a thickset Hungarian that spoke with broken English and was a behemoth of a man who wielded a set of menacing ice tongs seemingly effortlessly while he delivered our shimmering block of frozen splendor. Mr. Lazlo touted an elongated furrowed forehead with bushy brows and big bulging eyes. A thicket of wispy hair covered his rotund body and stuck out everywhere except for atop his balding head. His thick leather shoulder guards and apron were brown but stained dark because of the melting ice he carried. The rear of his wagon was packed and insulated with straw to keep the ice from melting before its delivery. Mr. Lazlo was probably harmless but he scared the heck out of not only me but every other kid in our neighborhood anyways. Every child around stayed clear of him and hid whenever they spotted his wagon coming down the road.

Of all of our possessions the one I considered the most valuable was our RCA Victor crystal radio that we kept in our living-room. After school or in the early evenings we would eagerly gather around it for good family fun. When Pittsburgh's KDKA syndicated station aired it became our main source of news and entertainment. KDKA broadcasted soap operas during the day which mom could enjoy while tending to her chores. There were adventure shows for the kiddies when they home from school and in the early evenings the station aired a number of variety shows and quality comedy.

We owned a black candlestick telephone that we kept sitting on the table equipped with operator accessibility and party line. Our ring was always two longs and a short and was distinctive. When answering the phone it was important to only pick up on your ring and not the neighbors. I'd learned that lesson by picking up on the wrong ring while my mother was outside. Because I had already picked up I tried to listen in on their conversation but somehow the person on the other end discovered the line had been compromised and was furious with me and began ranting for me to hang it up. By the tone and language it sounded very much like our foul mouthed neighbor, Jack Anthony.

Of all the household chores mom had, starching the crocheted doilies was by far her favorite and the most satisfying. She was like watching a mad scientist in action when in starching mode. Meticulously she would move from mold to mold manipulating the edges until her desired wavy pattern was achieved. The sticky solution she soaked them in could take hours to stiffen and dry but that didn't matter because just one ruffled disk could last a month, if we left them alone.

The entire production took up every inch of countertop and table space throughout the kitchen. Whenever the doilies gathered too much dust or went limp mom would round them up to redo them. After the doilies were properly washed she soaked them in a warm sugary solution for at least an hour before draping them individually over a collection of various sized mixing bowls spaced upside down all about the kitchen. As each sweetened crocheted disk began to harden mother manipulated the doilies transforming them into the decorative hilly rolled edge masterpieces she so enjoyed. Mom's doilies were then displayed throughout the house and adorned everything imaginable. They were placed under our candlestick phone, any and all lamps, clocks and she even had a special small oval shaped doily that rested beneath her crystal candy dish that she kept on the dresser in their bedroom. Understandably, mother would become very angry with us whenever she discovered one of her little works of art lying limp and unattractive beneath its intended object because one of us had sucked all the sugar out of her lacey beauties.

Mom's starched doilies reminded me of a stringy gob of rock candy and were usually a little dusty but delicious nonetheless. If ever Evelyn, James or I really needed something sweet and the candy dish was unavailable to us, mom's doilies could satisfy our sweet-tooth cravings.

Mom happened to be in the middle of her doilies project when one afternoon there was a knock at the door and because she was otherwise preoccupied she yelled for me to get the door. After peeking around the corner I saw a stranger wearing a suit and carrying a suitcase standing on our stoop which made me to run and fetch mom. Frustrated by being disturbed mom took off her apron, combed her fingers through her dark wavy hair and headed for the door where the man still stood waiting.

As she opened the door the stranger tipped his hat apologizing for the interruption. He introduced himself as a Hoover vacuum cleaner salesman and suggested he be allowed inside to demonstrate his amazing product. After gaining his entry one of the first questions asked was if mother had ever seen a vacuum cleaner before. She told him only in catalogs. That was when the man reached into his pocket and tossed a handful of dirt onto our area rug in the sitting room. Mom was furious and asked him what he thought he was doing. He assured her that there was no need to panic because his handy dandy sucking machine would clean up the mess in an instant.

"It better had." Mom said sternly.

The curious man sat his case down on the floor and opened it and began assembling his vacuum. I had to give it to him, this guy was slick as snot and twice as transparent but awe inspiringly quick. He had that complex contraption of his built in no time and was eager to demonstrate what his sucking machine was capable of doing.

The man went on to tell mother that Hoover's newly designed vacuum was not only attractive but that it only weighed ten pounds giving it easy maneuverability and could be stored anywhere. He claimed that because of all the work his machine could do, it would save mom a load of time and would therefore practically pay for itself and that a couple of our neighbors had already purchased from him and were very satisfied with the vacuum's performance. The man looked around the room for an electrical socket where he could plug his contraptions cord into the wall. As soon as he flipped the switch atop the tank and the engines deafening roar filled the room and he began shouting over the noise as though it were not a nuisance.

The effectiveness of his machine was impressive despite the noise and we were thoroughly entertained watching a man do woman's work. As the noise subsided ending the demo the salesman knelt down and began packing away his equipment and flattered mother on how clean she kept the house and how that he understood much work was involved in beating out a large carpet like ours.

"Okay how much is it?" mom asked growing tired of the spiel.

The salesman pulled out the paperwork and pointed to a figure. Mom balked. Her brief hesitation sent him into high gear pulling out all the stops. He was leading her to believe that she would be foolish if she didn't buy one and after baiting her, he threw in the hook and dragged her in. He proceeded to detail how the Hoover Company offered an easy payment plan designed to fit everyone's budget. I could see Mom was feeling the pressure and was wondering what she should do. Her excuse was that because it was such a large purchase she would have to discuss it with her husband. He then insisted that because she was so interested in his vacuum he would be willing to leave it with her for a free ten day trial and that if she was not completely satisfied, he would come back and pick it up and it would cost her nothing. Even though Mom was not sure it was a good idea the salesman walked out the door leaving the vacuum in its case claiming that he would be seeing her in ten days.

Mother used that vacuum cleaner every day during the trial period and by the time her ten days were up she'd made up her mind that she wanted one of her own. The salesman returned after ten days as promised. That salesman was great at his job having talked everyone of his clients that lived on our road into purchasing his sucking machine. I'd seen him making his rounds when I was outside playing in the neighborhood but I never saw him collect a single vacuum cleaner and he didn't collect ours either.

CHAPTER ELEVEN
TO SMOKE OR NOT TO SMOKE

In Pittsburgh there were a pocket of poor souls that lived in absolute squalor and my dearest friend and school chum, Jeffery Donald Davis, was one. Jeff was one of the poorest boy's I knew but what Jeff lacked in material goods he more than made up for in character. The Davis family eked out their living amid the shadows of some of the more lavish mansions strewn around Pittsburgh.

These luxurious manors were so grand in appearance they merited names like, "Clayton, Solitude, Rhu-Na-Craig, Lyndhurst, Beech wood and Grandview," to name only a few. While the Davis family home was neither palatial nor grand, it too merited a variety of names most of which were of a derogatory nature. Their two room shanty was meagerly furnished with a wrought iron bed and mattress, and old sofa where Jeff slept, one dresser, a kitchen table and a rummaged toilet that was stuck behind a curtain and useable because they had no running water. Their makeshift kitchen was disgusting and in disarray always.

Jeff's family was one of the few that still used an outhouse and even it looked to be falling apart and dilapidated.

Because their kitchen had no real sink or running water, they used a hand pump and used a basin to hold the water. There was a wooden trough rigged nearby that ran from the kitchen, through a hole in the wall, out to the backyard. This trough was used to dump such things as potato peels, rotting soup, egg shells and or any other garbage they wanted to discard, all of which washed down the chute with a basin full of dirty dish-water. The mucky, sudsy and rotting composition collected near the outhouse and smelled comparatively as offensive.

Because Jeff was poor he wore the same huge shirt that appeared to be a hand me down from his father. Jeff did his best to keep those shirttails tucked into his trousers but eventually they would work themselves free despite the thick leather belt he kept cinched tightly around his underfeed waist. His wide legged trousers were always bunched up and drooped sloppily about his hips because of how tightly he wore his belt.

Whenever Jeff rode his bike, which was often, he wore leather gaiters that buckled below his knees and again at his ankles to protect his pant-legs from getting stuck in his oily bike chain. The only time I'd seen Jeff frustrated was when that greasy chain would slip off the gear-cogs and fall limp around his pedals causing him to break his stride. Even then Jeff could hop off his bike, kneel down in the dirt and slip that greasy chain back on the cog in no time at all. He rode that old beat up bike everywhere. Jeff was tall for his age and still he appeared to short for his bike. The seat was supported by the two thick springs sat higher than his waist while the wide spread handlebars were nearly shoulder high on him. Jeff was like greased lightning and claimed that he never felt freer than when he rode his bike.

Jeff's father, Lyle Davis, was a well meaning lout that loved to take risks. As a gambler, Lyle would bet on anything that moved. While employed, Mr. Davis often lost his entire pay-packet making stupid wagers with the hope of striking it rich. Even when he did win he was never satisfied and would roll it over trying to win more. To avoid debt collectors, the

Davis's had moved around a lot. Jeff said he hated the deceit but that his father left them no choice and would come home in the evenings announcing that they needed to pack their bags so they could be gone before morning. All that happened prior to them moving Pittsburgh. Before coming to our area Jeff's father accidently ran into one of his old bookies and was severely beaten for it and was left for dead in an alley. Because of the severe beating he had suffered, Lyle Davis walked with a terrible limp and his speech was slightly slurred.

Like my father, Jeff's father liked his drink but he preferred gin, whiskey or good old moonshine over beer. They could barely afford food but he could always afford his daily bottle of booze and enough cigarettes to satisfy his habit thanks to Jeff. Because his father had sustained multiple injuries from the beating, to help ends meet Jeff made up a shoeshine kit. After school and on the weekends Jeff would ride his bike downtown and sit near the front of the old saloon that was next to the house of burlesque. Diligently Jeff would call out to every passerby and offer them a good shine for a nickel.

"Shoeshine, get your shoeshine," Jeff would bark.

Jeff's tenacity gained him the attention of a man that ran entertainment at the burlesque. He liked Jeff and not only would he get his shoes shined, he also sent him prospective clients. The man knew Jeff was struggling financially and so to help him out, asked Jeff if he wouldn't mind taking the stage to sing and dance between acts. Whatever the audience threw onto the stage was his. Jeff gave it a try but much of the clientele were cantankerous old men with no patience to see a young man singing his heart out when all they really wanted to see was the strippers. Those old grouches rarely tipped but once in awhile they would toss a coin up on the stage. They were often a rowdy crowd but the owner noticed that while Jeff took the stage he created a distraction that helped make his audience manageable in between acts. Jeff never made much but whatever money he did earn he shared with his folks.

Jeff did everything he could to support the family but his mother was not much better than his father. Her name was Prudence but she was anything but prudent. I would describe her as a slovenly woman, untidy in every way and so between her and her husband they made for an easy mark when I decided I wanted to give cigarettes a try. It looked so grown up to smoke but Jeff was not keen on the idea.

Sneaking around the Davis's house I picked up a cigarette and some matches and hid it in a fold of my dress until we were outside. When I showed Jeff what I'd done he was not happy but kept quiet. Wanting to find someplace private so I wouldn't get caught we headed down around the incline and hid there. While squatting down behind the wall I pulled out my illicit booty that I'd plundered from his folks and struck the match. Jeff was nervous and he kept peeking around the corner to make sure no one saw us.

When I lit the cigarette and took my first drag I coughed but after that I didn't inhale and it was alright. Jeff wanted no part of it and so I smoked it myself afterwards we parted company and I went home only to be found out by my mom. My first petty theft had backfired when unbeknownst to me I had a telltale bit of tobacco clinging to my front tooth and the smell of Chesterfield on my breath.

My mom went ballistic knowing I'd been smoking and boxed my ears but that was only the start. Every crime has a punishment and mine was to smoke as many cigarettes as she was going to give me with my head stuck under an army blanket which did not sound too bad but was. The musty smell of the woolen tent was only magnified by the noxious smoke that I was forced to inhale because of the blanket covering my head.

By the second cigarette that mother lit and handed to me to smoke I wanted to die. Feeling woozy everything began spinning out of control and my stomach flipped. Mother must have known I was struggling and when I couldn't take the smoke anymore I extinguished the cigarette on the bottom of my shoe and lay down before I fell down. I'm not sure how long I was left there but was relieved beyond measure when the blanket was pulled off and I saw the light in more ways than one. After swearing that I'd never smoke again I got up from the floor and went straight to bed and stayed there until the next morning.

The following Monday when I saw Jeff at school I told him all about what had happened and how I got caught. Jeff felt bad when he heard about my punishment but at the same time I could tell he was relieved. He knew I would never steal another cigarette from his folks again for as long as I lived and he was right.

CHAPTER TWELVE
FROM THE BEST DAY TO THE WORST

While Jeff made a little money singing, dancing and shining shoes I came up with, what I thought was a brilliant idea on how the two of us could make a little cash. It came to me that morning when father was reading the paper. He'd showed me a picture of a barefoot Asian man in white baggy pajama's breaking a thick board with his bare fist. The article was all about the martial arts. When I asked my dad why he was doing that father said he was a Karate instructer and that the man could also break those same boards with his bare feet as well. It all seemed very interesting and although I knew I would not be able to crack a board with my feet or hands I felt confident that I could snap a twig and set out to prove it.

Because it seemed a two person job I invited Jeff to partner up with me. I knew someone had to hold those sticks. According to my way of thinking, no adult would be able to resist a couple of cute kids performing feats of strength before their very eyes and they should be willing to pay for the experience. It seemed the perfect plan and Jeff was sweet enough to go along with me.

Between the two of us we had gathered a fair amount of some really dry sticks that we broke into manageable pieces about a foot in length. We found out early on that the greener twigs were too pliable and would bend before they would break and so in order to get the snapping effect we wanted, the sticks needed to be brittle. Because I didn't own a pair of white pajama's I wore a light colored dress and cinched it at the waist with a dark belt and wrapped a headband around my forehead to imitate the picture in the paper the best I could. With everything we needed in place we set out to dazzle our neighbors with our mastery of the mystical art of Karate.

The first person that opened their door stood dumfounded as we explained what we were doing there. I tried explaining that for the mere pittance of one cent she could witness me risk injury to my hand as I Karate chopped a stick that would be held by my faithful assistant and that the fee would of course be refunded if I failed. Jeff was such a good sport as he and I knocked every door for several blocks before we decided we should probably give up. Between the two of us we'd earned sixteen cents.

What I thought was a fabulous idea did not pan out as well as I had hoped. Jeff knew I was a little disappointed in my get rich quick scheme. He asked me how we should spend the money and I told him what I really wanted to do was try a banana split.

The local ice cream parlor had them but I knew they cost a little more than we'd earned. Because I'd had my heart set on it Jeff said that he could chip in the rest with some of the money he'd earned earlier in the week. Excitedly I agreed to let him help pay for our indulgence and we walked down to Klavon's where we ordered a special treat. Its lush décor was as gorgeous as the banana split was deliciously scrumptious. They had a solid marble soda fountain and counter top. The walls were made up of ornately carved wood panels, the floor was tiled and the ceiling was tinplated. Near the ceiling ran shelves displaying hundreds of assorted apothecary bottles of every shape and color. It was a thrill just to sit at the counter knowing we had enough money to place our order. "A banana split please." Jeff said as I spun back and forth on the stool excited.

"Just one?" the young man behind the counter asked while setting down the glass he was polishing.

"Yes please just one and two spoons," I added.

Anxiously we watched the young acne faced boy with the greasy hair and paper cap behind the counter assembling our delicious looking banana split and delicious it was. As soon as it was placed in front of us we dug in and ate every last melting bite. After sharing our banana split I shared something else and leaned over and gave Jeff my first kiss. Jeff was caught off guard but seemed pleased as his immediate response was for me to do it again to which I happily obliged. Jeff was to be the love of my life and I was just realizing how much I loved having him around. When I went home that day I was feeling on top the world but the feeling soon faded when I was told the news that my grandfather had died and that we would be leaving in the morning for his funeral.

The news of his demise came as such a shock we were all taken aback and our tears flowed like rain. A few weeks earlier Grandma had called with the news that Granddad had fallen and broken his hip but she assured us that he was fine and on the mend and so we postponed going down to see him. At the time of his accident grandma was out shopping with her daughter Catherine and daughter-in-law Ann and they had stopped at the local diner for a bite to eat before going home.

All the men folk were at work when granddad fell and so he was forced to lie on the damp hard floor for several hours before being rescued. While going down to their cellar he'd stepped on a dodgy board and fell. The cellar steps were steep, dark and with a loose board, proved to be dangerous. As soon as grandma walked into the kitchen to set her groceries bags down she sensed something was wrong but it was not until she heard him calling that she realized just how wrong. Uncle Morgan had just come in and was immediately sent to fetch the doctor. When the doctor came they were able between the two of them to get granddad up the stairs and into bed. The doctor said there was not much more he could do for him except manage his pain.

Granddad had broken plenty of bones while working the mines but when the doctor informed him that he would be bedridden until the facture healed and that it could take up to a year before he'd be able to walk again it broke his heart. Granddad loved his daily walk. Every morning before the cock crowed granddad made his way around the town. Being a creature of habit first he would always walk down the hill from the patch and into town where he would greet everyone he passed. After that he would trek over past the coke ovens and coalmine where he had worked for so many years and say hello to the men there. Then granddad usually headed up to the old baseball diamond for a quick stroll around the bases admiring the beautiful surroundings before heading back to the house for a good hardy breakfast which usually consisted of thick cut bacon, eggs and toast and a cup of coffee.

Everyone expected him to recover until he didn't. It was early March when the call came and we needed to take the long sad trip back to New Salem for his funeral. One of father's biggest regrets in life was that he did not go to New Salem when his dad had taken his fall and broke his hip. During that trip there would be no joy, no laughter and no singing. Silently we drove over the winding roads heading towards New Salem. Every once in a while I'd see dad wipe a tear off his cheek and sadly shake his head in unbelief that his father was really gone and I imagined how I would take the news if it was my father that had died.

Evelyn, James and I sat still and quiet in the rear seat not knowing what we should expect attending our first wake and funeral. All we thought about was seeing our granddad laid out in a coffin. James was confused and thought a wake was granddad waking up and joining us as usual. Evelyn and I tried to explain the night before that grandpa was not coming back because he was already in heaven. It was however the first time Evelyn, James or I would see a corpse and not just any corpse, it would be our beloved Grandfather. Without sharing my thoughts I believed that when we attended his funeral there would be a ghostly figure of my grandpa floating invisibly above the room watching over who had come and could listen to what they were saying about him. If his spirit was there, I think he would have been very pleased. The turnout was huge and everyone had only nice things to say about the man that was my granddad. Everyone complimented grandma on how well she was holding up under the tragic loss. As soon as we entered their house grandma came over and greeted us with a tearful kiss and a hug. It was all very sad but we got through it.

Within a few months of granddad's passing, grandma died too. Dad said she died of a broken heart because she missed granddad so much. Again we took that same somber trip to New Salem for another funeral. Dad told us that he imagined that as she walked through those pearly gates granddad and her baby boy Morgan was there to greet her with a loving hug and a kiss and what a grand reunion they would have. It was easier for us thinking about her death like that. To know she'd be with the son they'd lost so many years earlier and that knowing granddad was there with her and that he could walk without the use of a cane was a good thought. Grandma and grandpa had shared a good life and although they had some pretty rough times especially when they lost their son to the anthrax virus, they always had each other and from what dad said would have each other from then on. Granddad and grandma were fortunate in that their bond of love never wavered unlike my parents who by then were drifting farther and farther apart. After the loss of both his parents, father's drinking increased and so did their arguing.

Every family, when they have young ones running around, have emergency's come up and our family was no exception. If only dad had been around when the unsuspected happened. If we had his cool head guiding the way, things might not have been so bad and mother may have even forgiven his occasional drinking, but I doubt it. Dad's absences from home drove a deep wedge through the center of our mom's ever hardening heart.

One of those emergencies happened when Evelyn woke up one day complaining that she could not walk. She'd had a sore throat earlier in the week that turned into a bad headache and swollen joints. Mom looked her over and after feeling her brow realized that she was suffering from a low grade fever. It was not until mom tried to help Evelyn out of bed and she cried out in pain that mom knew how serious the matter was. Both Evelyn's knees and ankles were red and felt hot to the touch. They appeared to be swollen, stiff and sore. Without knowing exactly was the matter with her little girl mom panicked and ran all over the neighborhood begging for someone to give her a ride to the hospital.

Our neighbor, Mr. Anthony, ended up taking mom and Evelyn to the hospital where she was diagnosed with rheumatic fever. The doctor explained that rheumatic fever was very serious and that it would give Evelyn problems for the rest of her life. Besides the arthritic pain she would have to endure, there had been permanent damage done to her heart. Evelyn could expect to suffer other symptoms as well such as a shortness of breath, nosebleeds and periodic rashes. Needless to say the diagnosis was serious and because father wasn't home when it happened and she had to beg a neighbor for a ride to the hospital she never forgave him. Evelyn remained in hospital for over a week and when she did come home she was weak as a kitten and needed complete bed rest for close to a month. After that she was forbidden to run for an entire year. The doctor warned it would be dangerous for her to over exert herself in any way.

Evelyn was careful and minded all the doctor's instructions by refusing to run, jump or walk fast. We worried that her heart might give out and she would die. It was just as well that the rheumatic fever happened to Evelyn and not me because I didn't think I could have followed our doctor's advice so easily.

CHAPTER THIRTEEN
OUR CAR

Jeff Davis had been so poor he considered my family well off. In all reality, we weren't, or at least I didn't think so. According to Jeff anyone with food in the pantry and a car in the driveway were rich. We may not have been wealthy but we were considered members of Pittsburgh's middle class, even though I believe we landed on the lower end of middle as there were plenty of Pittsburghers who had much more than us. Some of them were so rich they didn't need to even keep track of what they spent or what they did. They were the ones who were in need of accountants and boards of people to handle their finances and make their investments for them to keep them living the lifestyle they'd grown accustom too. Pittsburgh had its fair share of self made millionaires as well as those who were born into wealth. The old money aristocrats looked down upon not only the new money folks but on the working class people as well.

There were two girls in the neighborhood whose parents had what my folks called, "Real money." They would come into our part of town strutting as though they were royalty and to be bowed down too. As my friend Jeff so succinctly put it, their farts stunk just as much as ours and probably more because of the fancy food they ate. Things like caviar, lobster, thick juicy steaks and such may not have been on their menu every night but at least they had the opportunity to partake in the finer things of life. Every time I saw them coming around I wanted to scream. Both Nelly and Annabelle attended the same private school. It always got up my nose whenever they showed up sporting their frilly little dresses, ruffled socks and shinny patent leather shoes. They were afforded the luxury of wearing a different dress every day unlike me and my sister who had to use the same dresses repeatedly. Where Nelly was blonde Annabelle had dark hair. Their long shining ringlets bounced rhythmically and were hypnotic as they pranced side by side along the street. They always sported a matching hair ribbon neatly tied in bow positioned at a rakish angle above their left ear.

Whenever they walked by our house they would be chuckling and jabbing each other in the ribs like we were deemed unworthy to gaze upon their charm. I could only imagine what they might do if they ever walked past Jeff's house and saw the conditions he lived in but his was one neighborhood they would never have ventured into, not even on a dare. They spotted me once helping my father to start our car. Dad saw them coming and took off his cap and bowed politely greeting them with a, "Good day ladies."

The pair of them rudely looked at each other as though my father had worms growing out of his ears and laughingly they ran off making fun. It made me feel like picking up a rock and chucking it at their oversized heads. Father paid them no mind and I knew he would want me to do the same no matter how hard it was.

Our automobile was a hand cranked Model T that my father adored. He always boasted that, "Nothing ran like a Ford," and credited Henry Ford for putting America on wheels. Our Model T was sturdy, economical and easy to drive once you got it started. It ran on a four-cylinder 2892-cc engine and had a whopping 20 horsepower at its disposal producing 1,500 rpm, that could bring its top speed to over 37 miles per hour. Dad enjoyed the freedom our Tin-Lizzie provided. When I was really young dad would sometimes hold me in his lap so I could steer as he worked the gas and the break. When I was older he'd sometimes allow me to guild the steering wheel while sitting next to him.

We may have been able to purchase a newer model car but father was perfectly content with the one we had claiming he would keep it until it disintegrated to the point he could brush it into a dustpan. Dad only drove the car on occasion. Usually he hopped the local trolley for transport back and forth into town. It was a joy seeing him running down the street yelling to the trolley driver, "Slow down I'm coming." They never did slow down but I'd never seen father miss it either. At the last second father would reach out and grab hold onto the guard-rail near the rear entrance of the trolley and swing himself up onto the loading step. Teasingly he would dangle off the end darning his cap and bowing good-bye to me as the trolley rolled out of view. He could always put a smile on my face.

One day while my father was at the mill, I decided to show off some of the things he'd taught me about the car to my friend Jeff. My mom had already started her doily project and so I knew she would be tied up in the house for at least a few hours giving me plenty of time to do my demonstration. After pointing out how easy the car was to drive I convinced Jeff that if he helped me we'd be able to start it and if we were quick about it we could drive it around the block and have it back in the driveway in no time.

My suggestion tempted him as I made it sound like a proper adventure with no fear of us getting caught. Talking Jeff into it was easy and to put some icing on the cake, I told him he'd be the one driving because I was too short and couldn't reach the peddles. As Jeff proudly sat behind the steering wheel I pointed out what each peddle was for and what the different gadgets on the dashboard meant and even though I'd never personally driven without my father, I felt confident that because Jeff had long legs he'd be a perfect cohort. I knew steering the car was easy as I had done it so many times before. Jeff was ecstatic and grinned wildly as he played with the steering wheel jerking it back and forth in anticipation of me giving him his first driving lesson.

The emergency hand brake was already set and I showed Jeff how to engage the clutch while I put the shifter into neutral. With the shifter in place I raised the left spark lever to the top position and lowered the throttle lever until I saw the gas pedal move a smidge, just as my father had always done. After instructing Jeff to pull the choke out I stepped in the front of the car and turned the crank after sliding the lever into its place underneath the radiator grill.

When Jeff was ready I jerked it as hard as I could until I felt the rod catch the lower position just left of center. Looking up at Jeff through the windscreen I signaled for him to get ready and grasped that crank with both hands and after taking a deep breath and while saying a little prayer I positioned the crank up and to my great surprise it worked and the crank dropped into the ready position for the starting just like it did for my dad.

Everything was going according to plan and with great excitement building I cranked it again and when I smelt the gas flowing into the carburetor I knew I had done everything right. I called for Jeff to release the choke and turn on the ignition which he did. All I needed to do then was give her one last, fast crank and she should start and we would be on our way. It was exhilarating and although I'd only planned on driving the car once around the block I didn't plan on what happened next. The final crank made the car jump and backfire with a loud boom. A thick plume of black smoke popped out of the tailpipe which scared the devil out of me and Jeff.

There was no way my mother had not heard what just happened and so I told Jeff to "Cheese It!" which he did and in the nick of time, I might add, because my mother raced onto the scene from one direction as Jeff exited the scene going the other way. There I stood with the driver's door wide open and the starting crank still suspended from the front of the car. Mother stood in the driveway slightly bent over clutching her side and out of breath panting before the smoke cleared.

I was petrified and with good reason too. Mother lunged in my direction pulling off her shoe in the process and began beating me with its heel. When I tried to protect myself from the blows it only infuriated her further and I swore I heard mother backfire a couple of times like the car had as she wielded that heavy shoe trying her best to clock me good and then came the threat…"Just you wait till your father gets home!" as she dragged me into the house by my hair ordering me to shut-up and stop crying or she would give me something to cry about. As soon as Mom went into the pantry I knew she was going for that darn mason jar of popcorn kernels and sure enough I was right. I watched, between sobs and sniffles as she poured a neat little pile in the corner on the linoleum floor and then shoved me onto them forcing my nose to the wall and my knees onto those digging hulls.

Every once in a while I would hear her shout out a warning for me, that I had better not to move an inch. Both my mom and those darn kernels had made their point. From my position I couldn't see if she was still in the kitchen but I swore I could feel her glare on my back. Nevertheless I stayed put. Those dog-gone seeds hurt like the dickens as the hard pointy bits gouged deeply into skin and the linoleum. I had no idea how long my mom would make me stay there. If I had to wait there until my father came home I could have been there all night.

Everyone knew my dad liked his beer and often spent hours at a local bar when he got off work. My dad's drinking had been a bone of contention between my parents for as long as I could remember but I had hope that, that night might be one of those rare occasions when he would come straight home after work to rescue me from "His Brides" wrath. His bride was a pet name he used for my mom, always after he'd had too much to drink. Mother hated it when he called her, "His Bride." There was no telling on how long she would keep me kneeling in the corner but it was well after my knees had gone numb and I'd fallen asleep. After a number of hours even my mom had grown tired of waiting for him and granted me a reluctant reprieve and shooed me off to bed.

My knees were dimpled and stiff and I had trouble walking. Mother had two things to stew over, me trying to drive the car and father being late again. By the time dad did get home he too was stewed but he with ale and mother with ire. I'd hoped that dad might overlook what I had done and that my punishment had already been met between the shoe beating, the popcorn corner and the threats. The whole episode was after all a learning experience and again I had diverted mom's wrath away from him and had hope he might appreciate it.

Because of father's hours at the mill I did not see him until the weekend. That was when he advised me that we were going to the woods of which I was excited about thinking I was to be rewarded for being a good daughter. James and Evelyn wanted to go as well, but they were not invited on that particular trip making me feel special. Father grabbed me, his hat and his ten gauge double barrel shotgun and off we went into the woods. Mother had either instructed him to kill me or he was going to teach me how to shoot and because I knew father would never hurt me I was excited.

The smog hung heavily in the field that day as we made our way through the high grass and into the open glen opposite the woods. Father marched grandly and with purpose as I walked behind him trying to keep up with his long strides. His tall willowy form cut a striking image as he followed the set path into the forest where he pointed out a spot where a hobo had built a makeshift shelter in a clearing.

After assuring that the campground was empty of drifters father gathered some of the refuse he'd found lying around and set up a target for practice. There was an old tree stump where father positioned a tin can and after snapping open and loading the twin barrels father snapped it shut and handed me the gun. It was much heavier than I imagined and I had a hard time holding it straight. I didn't know if I could shoot it but dad said that if I thought I was old enough to drive his car I was surely old enough to handle a shotgun and that shooting was easier than driving and that all I needed to do was aim and pull the triggers.

Dad reached over taking off the safety and setting the triggers to go off together firing both barrels at once. Nervously excited and feeling very grown up I took aim and pulled the trigger. The guns strong recoil knocked me backwards and the hard ground came up fast to meet my behind. Dad chuckled and picked up the gun before helping me up inspected his gun pulling out a clump of grass from the sight as the barrels were hot and still smoking. Holding back the tears I rubbed my aching shoulder.

Dad said that I was knocked down because I'd failed to press the butt of the gun tightly to my shoulder and that he saw what was going to happen but that he was trying to teach me a lesson and my lesson was that I wasn't a big as I thought I was and my father was right. I should never have tried to drive the car.

Luckily, for Jeff, my folks never did find out that he was an accomplice that day. They didn't ask and I didn't tell. The whole thing was my idea and there was no reason to drag my friends name into it. When I told Jeff about my punishment he thought it sounded like fun and it kind of was except for my sore shoulder. The fact that we were together when we tried to drive the car remained our little secret.

CHAPTER FOURTEEN
MAJOR

In those days pets were considered something of a luxury. My father loved animals and while mother respected them, she never considered entertaining one as a pet. Because mother was raised on an Indian reservation she grew to believe that animals were just that, animals, nothing more and nothing less. They belonged outside and free. For her they had their purpose. Cats, for instance, were to keep the rodent population at bay and the only good dog was a herder. Since mother never hid how she felt about pets Evelyn, James and I were shocked the day we came home from school only to discover we had a puppy running around the house and it was ours. Even mother seemed to be beaming with joy over our latest addition to the family. The prancing golden pup was named Major.

Major, it turned out, was a three month old rambunctious fur balled collie. He had a long extended tapered nose that jetted out in front of his fussily tufted ears and white collar befitting a lion's mane. We thought him a wonderful surprise and could not wait to play with him. Evelyn, James and I fell in love with Major the second we laid eyes on him. He was a beautiful dog that liked to follow us everywhere, that is, everywhere except home. We'd only had Major for three months when we lost him.

Evelyn and I had gone down the street to play with the Donavan girls, Marcy and Lisa and without realizing it James and Major had followed us. While they eventually made it over to where we were, James and Major had made a few stops along the way and turned up just as an argument had erupted between Lisa Donavan and their neighbor, Nancy Clemens. All of us went to the same school and even though Nancy was the oldest of our little group, we were in the same class. Among the Clemens clan Nancy was their oldest girl and stuck out like a sore thumb. The rest of her family took after their father who was short and of a ruddy complexion. The rest of the Clemens siblings had dark hair and eyes whereas Nancy was tall, fair skinned and had freckles and was cute as a button like her mother.

After a squabble started between Nancy and Lisa that was getting loud we were sent home. By then Evelyn and I were hungry and because we'd been playing for hours figured our supper would be about ready and it was. Evelyn, James and I ran into the house and squished our bodies around the bathroom sink grappling with the one bar of soap. From hand to hand we passed the soap while lightly rinsing the suds under the running water before turning off the spigot and soiling the then dirty towel drying our hands before heading for the table to get some grub. As mother doled out the food she told us to settle down and behave.

"Where's Major?" She inquired while plopping down a heaping spoonful of mashed potatoes on my plate.

Now I had no idea where Major was and at the time I had been so hungry I really didn't care.

"I dah-know?" I replied smugly before digging into my steamy hot mashed potatoes.

Mother was furious with my caviler attitude and jerked my plate out from in front of me and ordered me to go find him. I wasn't the one that lost the dog and so I didn't know why I was the one that had to go look for him but I knew better than to open my mouth in protest and left. After going outside I started my search in our own backyard but he wasn't there. Then I walked over towards Marcy and Lisa's calling his name all the way but there was no site of him. The longer I called his name without seeing him come running the lower I felt fearing this was not going to end well for any of us. Our Major was gone and I had to go home and face the music.

"Well, did you find him?"Mom asked as soon as I walked in the door.

After shrugging my shoulders and shaking my head no, mom went mad and slapped me across the face insisting I had been careless. After I was scolded I was sent to bed without my supper and Evelyn was made to join me but she had already eaten before I got back. James was excused from being punished. The next day mother was in an extremely bad mood as our Major had not returned in the night. When I told Jeff what had happened and that we'd lost our dog he came up with a great idea and suggested that we make up some lost dog posters and scatter them around town which we did. Mom knew we'd never see our, Major, again but when over a week past without a single response to our posters or our door knocking campaign, I believed it too. Mom kept rubbing it in claiming that, because of us, "somebody got themselves a really good dog," which made us feel terrible about losing him. Whenever I'd see a collie anywhere I wondered if it was our lost Major. I think mom was right; somebody got themselves a really good dog.

Within a month of the, "Major," episode, while Jeff and I were walking home from his house we happened onto a yard where there were a couple of cute and playful roly-poly puppies running around. Because I'd become so excited seeing them and because Jeff knew the man and often talked to him whenever he passed he asked if we could come see his puppies. Overjoyed that he'd asked and that we'd gained permission I clutched Jeff's arm excitedly as we entered the yard. As soon as I sat down on the ground the entire litter came running up to me tripping clumsily over their nubby little legs. They looked so funny and I laughed as I happily picked up the first pup that jumped on me. As I held it up it licked my face and kicked its paws excitedly. Its puppy breath reminded me of the hash my mom sometimes cooked for us and I was having a wonderful time when the man said that they were the last of the litter and that I could take one home if I wanted. He made Jeff the same offer and said he too could have a pup but Jeff declined knowing his family could not afford another mouth to feed.

All I was thinking was that a brand new pup could make up for losing Major and so, acting as an emissary for our family, I chose the one that I thought was the pick of the litter, though it was a tough decision. Three of the pups were male and the other two were female, I chose one of the females. She was gorgeous and sweet and her wide soft paws that drooped aimlessly as I proudly carried her to her new home. I really thought that mother would be as thrilled as I was but she wasn't. Maybe it was because I'd not asked first or maybe it was because I was the one that found her either way the mistake was mine.

When I walked into the kitchen to show off our new pup to mom I was immediately ordered me to take the "mutt" back to wherever it came from. It was crushing news and I was gutted but because it was getting late and supper was ready I was allowed to keep the puppy until the next day.

I was really dreading the thought of taking her back but was glad that I could keep her for the night and took her to our bedroom so I could play with her. Watching her darting around the floor gave me an idea for the perfect name. Mother had warned me not to get too attached to her but it was already too late. She was so cute and I felt so lucky to have found her that I named the pup Star and made my wish upon her that she would be mine to keep.

Knowing that my father liked dogs more than my mom it did cross my mind that if he got home early enough I might be able to ask him about Star and maybe he could convince mom that she would be a nice pet for us.

When Evelyn and James saw the puppy we put our heads together and began the three P's. Playing, plotting and praying. Star proved to be wildly entertaining and to play a trick on her we placed a table mirror on the floor so she could see her reflection. Star went crazy and started yapping out a series of dainty little barks while pawing and biting at the mirror. Being afraid the yapping would anger mother we decided we should put the mirror away. I waved her own tail in her face until round and round she went chasing it until she tripped and fell over on her side. It was great fun watching what Star would do next.

As soon as we heard the side door slam we got excited knowing our father had come home. James and Evelyn got up from the floor to greet our father but I'd already cautioned them to wait until he'd had chance to eat before we bombarded him with questions about Star and if we could keep her. They agreed and as a united front we stayed in our room and let him and mom talk. The dog subject did not come up and father was able to eat his supper in peace. Everything was quiet and as we peeked through the doorway we could see mom starting to wash some dishes. That's when we heard dad call out, "Where's my family?" and we came running with the pup in tow.

"Whoa, whoa, what's this?" Dad asked picking the pup up off the floor.

"It's Star." We chirped in unison.

"Well hello Star, where'd you come from?"

"She's a girl daddy"

Dad took a look underneath and said, "Yup, looks like your right. Who named her Star?"

"Um, I kinda did," I said taking the credit.

Mother interrupted saying, "It has no name because it's going back in the morning."

"She sure is a pretty pup and smart too." Father said already teaching her how to sit and shake.

"Her coloring reminds me of taffy. Hey that's what we should call her, Taffy. Star sounds too much like a boy's name," father continued.

"I already said we're not calling her anything because she's going back in the morning!" Mom said clarifying the situation.

As soon as our father changed the pup's name and began arguing in her defense, I knew we had him. It wasn't a huge argument and mother soon gave in with the provision that the dog was to be my responsibility, not hers and that Taffy would have to be chained outside. When I went to bed that night I thanked my lucky, "Star" even though from then on she would be known as Taffy.

Within the week of having her, father built Taffy a proper doghouse. It was one project that dad let me help with. He explained that the house needed to be small so she could conserve her heat when it got cold outside. I asked him if we could bring her inside when it got really cold and he said that would be up to mom but that he thought Taffy would be alright outside as long as we kept enough straw on hand to insulate the doghouse. Taffy barked for a couple of hours when she was first put on the chain but then she settled down and went into the doghouse for the night. As she grew the chain wore down a circular path in the lawn. Taffy would get so excited whenever we went out to free her so she could play.

On a dark winter's night while we were all sitting around the kitchen table talking my father noticed Taffy's dish on the floor and asked if I'd fed her already. I had in fact forgotten to feed her that day and felt terrible about it. Dad assured me that Taffy wouldn't starve in a day but that she did need to be fed and that she also needed fresh water. After grabbing her dish and all the table scraps I went to go out the side door to feed her when I paused. It had really gotten dark and I was a little afraid. Because father understood he suggested that I go into the car and turn on the headlights. He explained that the bright beams would light a path out to the doghouse but he warned me that I needed to shut them off when I was done or else his battery would go flat by the morning. It sounded like such a good idea to me and I remember thinking how clever my father was for thinking of it. After rinsing out an empty milk bottle and filling it with fresh water I headed out the door and to the car where I turned on the headlights lighting the way for me. Taffy was very excited to see me that night and I apologized to her for my error and gave her some extra attention while she wolfed down her food emptying her dish. After refreshing her water and giving her a good dog pat on her head I picked up her dish and walked back to dad's car to shut off the headlights. When I reached for the door handle dad grabbed my hand through the open window and shouted out a heart stopping, "Boo!" causing me to scream out, jump backwards falling to the ground in fear for my life.

By then father was laughing so hard over his perfectly timed prank he was having a difficult time getting out of the backseat so he could help me. It took a second to realize what had happened and it took me some time to appreciate the humor of his prank but because of what he'd done I never forgot to feed Taffy again. She was a sweet dog and we loved her.

CHAPTER FIFTEEN
PUT A CORK IN IT

An Irish family with the name of Cork, lived across the street from me. They were a rowdy bunch that fought constantly over everything imaginable. What little they had could only be stretched so far and so it became a family issue for them to get to whatever they wanted first, before their many siblings could. They became a family of first. First to the table, first to the toilet, first to the clothesline became their goal in life.

The two eldest Cork boys, Pat and Mick, used to duke it out in the yard over which one got to wear the one clean shirt that fit them the best. Their fights were especially intense after they hit puberty and became interested in impressing the local young ladies. Their second eldest daughter, Colleen, was sent away as soon as an unexplainable but noticeable bump in her tummy started growing and it was about that time that my mother forbade me and Evelyn from associating with any of them. We were told that if we ever saw one of the Cork's walking towards us we were to cross over and walk on the opposite side to avoid their immoral contamination.

Six of their thirteen children went to school with Evelyn, James and I while the older ones had already left school by the time we attended. Beth was Evelyn's age, Frank was my age and little Kelly Ann was the same age as our James. Beth Cork was an untidy little girl with flyaway strawberry-blonde wavy hair, green eyes and crusty eyelashes. Beth had so many freckles they clumped together in spots making some of them quite large while others were mere specks. Beth's one brother, Frank, looked a great deal like her, crusty eyelashes and all.

The difference between Frank and Beth, besides their gender, was that his head was kept shaved because of a bout the family had with lice. Beth and the rest of their clan shared in the lice outbreak but they refused to shave their hair and opted to slather their heads with lard to get rid of them. Beth and Frank's relationship was odd to say the least. They behaved as though they were boyfriend and girlfriend instead of brother and sister.

A year or so before Colleen was sent away, Beth Cork tried to befriend me despite the fact she was closer to Evelyn's age than mine. Beth had worked out that Evelyn was a goodie-two-shoe and possessed more sense than me and it was just as well because Beth was not the kind of girl Evelyn would have run around with anyhow. Finding out that my sister was absolutely right about Beth Cork did not take me long either.

Beth had invited me to come into their backyard where we could play. When I got there Beth told me she wanted to show me something and took me to their shed. When she opened the door her brother Frank was already inside waiting for us. I had a sinking feeling that something wasn't right but I was curious about what they were up to and why they wanted me there. Their shed was hot, dark and dusty and gave me the creeps. It had a dirt floor and the walls, rafters and contents were covered with hanging cobwebs and grime. There was just enough light seeping in through the wooden slats to see what was going on.

Once inside their house of horrors Beth asked me to close my eyes and insisted I kept them shut until they were ready. Beth was playfully giggling and I could hear some rustling in the background before they told me that I could open my eyes. There the two of them stood posed in their "altogether" without an ounce of shame and if that wasn't shocking enough what they did next was unbelievable and wrong. Beth and Frank blocked my escape and after Frank relieved himself on the ground Beth licked the last little drop from his penis and asked me if I wanted to have a go at it. My jaw dropped as I pushed past them and ran home never to spill a word about the troubling exhibition I'd just witnessed in their shed across the street. I never went back. The depravity of their minds made me feel sick and dirty and I almost threw-up. It would be one encounter that I never spoke of to anyone, especially Jeff. My world was fast changing and out of control and I rued the day that I joined them in their shed. It's a funny thing about the loss of innocence, once it's gone you can never get it back and I had lost some of mine that day and I knew it.

My next encounter with Beth and Frank Cork happened some time later. Jeff and I were busy playing in my front yard and were minding our own business when Frank and Beth came sauntering over and stood in front of my house on the sidewalk. Catching them out of the corner of my eye I wondered what they were up to this time. Again I heard Beth giggle which made me shudder a little before she called the two of us over to show us something. My first thought was here I go again but since Jeff was with me and we were in my yard I figured it would be alright to see what they were up to. Jeff's presence always felt safe and so because of that together we went to them to see what was going on. That was when Frank curiously sat down on the ground in front of us and began taking off his shoes and socks to proudly display his freshly painted toenails. Jeff thought it was funny and I was just glad that was all he wanted to show us.

We probably should not have engaged them in conversation but Jeff was curious and blurted out the question as to who painted his toenails?

"Beth did," Frank boasted pointing to his sister.

"Wha'd ya lead'er do that for?" Jeff questioned.

"Ain't dey Purdy." Frank countered without answering why.

"For a girl," I said before grabbing Jeff's arm and turning him to walk away uninterested as I thought he looked ridiculous but at least it wasn't obscene.

Beth took umbrage at me turning by back on them and picked up a rock she'd found lying in the road and flung it at me hitting me squarely in the back of my head. The rock left a huge knot and a bleeding gash. While I ran into the house bawling, Jeff ran after Beth who had made it home and locked herself inside. Frank was frantically grappling to get his shoes back on so he could escape too. Frank hadn't thrown the rock and so Jeff left him there and came to our backdoor to check on me. Mother had been in the middle of cleaning the kitchen when I ran in blubbering and holding the back of my head.

"What on earth?" She asked dropping her scrub brush and getting up from her knees. By then I was practically hysterical and between blubbering sobs I managed to get out the name Beth Cork. When my mom heard the name Cork and felt the back of my head she went mad and raced to our phone so she could call the police.

The rock had lacerated my head which was bleeding profusely. Mom ran a washrag under the spigot and handed it to me to hold over the bump to help stop the bleeding. That was when I felt the bump for the first time and I realized how much it had swollen. Mother compared it to a goose egg when she was reporting the incident to the police. After the phone call and while we waited for the police to arrive mother went to the icebox and chipped away at the block to collect some shavings that she gathered and wrapped into a clean towel. She saved the bloody cloth for evidence.

As I was holding the ice to my bump I saw Jeff peering in through the screen. Just knowing he was there made me feel some better and I waved for him to come inside, which he did. Jeff looked like he was going to faint when I lifted the icepack and showed him my bloody knot. Mom yelled at me to keep icing it. She said that the police were on their way. Jeff handed my mom the very rock that Beth used and informed her that Beth and Frank were across the street hiding out in their house. Mom thanked him for retrieving the evidence and put it with the bloody cloth before sending him home. Jeff didn't want to leave me, but mother insisted telling him that I would be alright and that he could come back by after everything settled down.

The policeman dispatched was a short but pleasant looking bloke touting a broad mustache and pronounced sideburns. Mother was raging mad by then and flung the door open dragging me by my arm and shoving me out on the porch in front of her and made the officer feel the back of my head. While the officer was having a little look and a feel of my head I spied around his waistcoat only to see a shift in the drapes across the way. By then I had stopped crying but felt a few fake sobs were in order, hoping my tears would heap some insult to my injury getting Beth in more trouble for what she'd done.

Unlike the time in their shed, they were probably both pissing their pants when they saw the copper at our front door talking to my mom. The officer agreed that it was a nasty bump and assured my mother that he would go over and talk to their parents about the incident. My mom told him that it would do no good and that Mr. and Mrs. Cork were drunks and could care less about what their little hoodlums were up to.

"That scruffy little brat could have killed my Rosie. Look at the size of this damn rock!" Mom insisted waving Beth's weapon of choice under his nose.

"Like I said, I'll make a report and have a word with her folks."

We watched as the officer walked across the street and went inside. Mother was right about them not caring and nothing came of the report. The officer went over and spoke to Beth and Franks parents but no apology was forthcoming.

There would be no more dealings with Beth Cork who turned out to be one of those girls that matured early and loved showing off her newly developed breast to as many of the local boys that would come over to see them and come they did. As soon as the word got out that Beth Cork would bare her breast, boys from all over the countryside rode into the neighborhood for a sneak-peek. Larry Horvath was one of those boys that had heard the rumors of Beth Corks big booby show extraordinaire. Larry traveled by bicycle over eight miles to get a private viewing. By the time he rode up our street and located her house the poor boy was over so overheated that I thought he might faint and offered him a cool drink of water. Some of the water he drank but most of it he poured over his head. That was when he asked me if I knew where Beth Cork lived. As soon as he asked I knew why he came and pointed to the Cork house across the way.

"Thanks," he said excitedly dropping his bike in our yard and running across the street to knock her door. Frank opened the door and told the boy that his sister was not at home. Poor Larry looked heartbroken when he came back to my yard to collect his bike. He asked if I had any idea where Beth might be and so I told him that she often hung out down around the local ice cream parlor and that if he bought her a treat she would be ever so grateful and I was thinking that for his kindness she would gladly treat him to a peek. Excited to know he might have a second chance Larry hopped back onto his bike and headed for Pittsburgh's downtown district in search of Beth Corks, uncorked twin deities in all their glory but Beth had just left by the time Larry arrived. The poor boy began asking around where Beth might be. Some folks said she had been seen in Darlington's Diner around lunch time, so he rode his bike over to the local diner but there was no sign of Beth Cork at Darlington's.

"Have you seen Beth Cork?" Larry asked a passerby anxiously.

"Ah you just missed her." A young man told him, having heard the rumors swirling around Miss Cork's antics.

"Do you know where she went?" Larry inquired.

"Yeah, she said she was headed down to Triangle between Diamond and Sixth." He replied, jerking the unsuspecting Larry around, having had no idea where Beth Cork was, but he knew her reputation and why the winded boy was so anxious to find her.

Larry hopped back onto his bike and headed down the road in search of his destiny. Poor Larry was acting like a deer mesmerized by a vehicle's headlamps at dusk and Larry seemed transfixed by the very thought of seeing Beth's. Larry rode that darn bike all over the valley hither and yarn and as folklore had it, he is probably still peddling in pursuit of the elusive Beth Cork and her legendary "Grand Tetons'."

The Illinois Central may have had their famous Casey Jones conducting the train and blowing his whistle but we in Pittsburgher had own Larry Horvath, a bike riding fool that peddled his way into our town's annuals of time and was a local legend in his own right.

It was rumored that on a warm moonlit night you could sometimes hear the echo of Larry's bicycle tires roaming the hills in search of Beth Cork's peep show.

CHAPTER SIXTEEN
OUR BELOVED AUNT RUBY

On a gray September morning while Evelyn and James were still sleeping I awoke with a start and the feeling of dread. I couldn't shake the feeling that something terrible was about to happen. Unlike mother's premonitions and her unexplained knocks on the wall I wasn't sure what had caused me to wake up or why I felt the way I was but before I could even think about laying back down I knew I should get up and investigate.

The house was eerily quiet as I walked out of our room and into the hallway. Figuring dad was already on his way to the mill I peeked into my parent's room to make sure mom was alright but their bed was empty which seemed odd. There were no lights turned on anywhere in the house and so I stepped into the kitchen to see if mother was in there but she wasn't. With my worry mounting there was no point in going back to bed and so I decided that I should brew a pot of coffee and wait. I'd hoped mother was visiting a neighbor for some inexplicable reason and after noticing a few unwashed dishes in the sink I decided that I would wash them to occupy my time until her return. I'd hoped that a nice cup of coffee and the dishes washed would please her and so as I started to make the coffee and while empting the dregs and rinsing the old grounds left in the basket I glanced out of the window into the backyard.

The fog was especially thick that day and as my eyes adjusted to the hazy mist I could just about make out a troubling image standing atop father's woodshed. Dropping what I was doing I raced outside only to find the image I saw from in the house was my mother perched on the edge of the roof and she appeared to be contemplating a jump. Mumbling and as if in a trance mother teetered on the edge. Not knowing what she could have been doing up there I called out for her to come down but she just gazed into space like she didn't hear me. While in her trancelike state and without saying a word to my horror mother jumped and crumbled on the ground sobbing hysterically before me.

Running over to her I bent down and knelt beside her. It was then she realized I was there as she swatted at me with her hand and ordered me to leave her alone and get back inside. Worried about her wellbeing and so despite her trying to shoo me away I stayed put and refused to go without her. After a deep and tearful sigh mother reached out as I helped her to her feet. The sun was just beginning to peek above the surrounding hills and I heard our milkman delivering our two quarts. Thankfully he was so busy with his route he did not see us or what was going on. Mother looked weak and frail from her ordeal and leaned on me for guidance as we went back inside together.

When we got to the kitchen table I sat mother down and told her that I would finish the pot of coffee I'd only started earlier. While the coffee perked she starred off into space. Every now and then she shook her head wiped a tear from her cheek and mumbled something incoherently. Mother's breakdown was disturbing and I did not want Evelyn and James to see her like that and so when I heard them stirring I sent them on an errand to borrow some sugar from a neighbor. When they got back I told them that I'd just mopped the floors and that they should go play outside for a while. By then mother had come to her senses and thanked me for taking the initiative of getting James and Evelyn out of the way. The coffee was ready and I poured her a cup and set the sugar bowl and milk within her reach but she chose to drink it black that day.

While mom sipped her coffee she commented that I was growing up fine and invited me to pour myself a cup of coffee and join her and so I did. I couldn't drink mine black and so I added a level spoonful of sugar and a little bit of milk which helped cool it down but it was still too hot for me to enjoy and so I blew on it. We'd sat there for a little while before mom began opening up as to why she'd jumped off the roof. What she told me was shocking but the way she told me made me feel sorry for her. It seemed she had gone to the doctor and it had been confirmed that she was expecting.

"Expecting what?" I asked still blowing on the rim of my cup.

Mom paused for a moment and took a deep shameful sigh, "A baby."

Her answer made me scorch the roof of my mouth when I inadvertently took a large gulp of my hot coffee. My reaction made mother go quiet again and she sat at the table and stared off into space. Her frailties were overwhelming and so I decided it was not the time to question her any further and so I left her to her thoughts and stood up and went over to the sink and busied myself washing the dishes I'd planned on washing before all hell broke loose. Without knowing what to say, I said nothing but my mind was running a mile a minute and I wondered if dad knew what was going on and that we were going to have an addition to the family as long as mother didn't succeed in stopping it from happening.

Mother's feeble attempt to end her pregnancy had fortunately failed and so because of that I kept what I knew about her jumping off the roof to myself. Whether she made any other tries to stop the impending birth I knew not, but if there were any, they too were unsuccessful. Within six weeks of the roof incident her baby bump started to show itself and everyone knew there would be another mouth to feed in the Evan's household. Seeing mothers stomach growing made me to realize why our neighbor, Colleen Cork, had moved away all those years ago. Colleen was unmarried at the time and a scandal of that proportion would have been ferocious and I was thankful that at least our mom was married and so her pregnancy would be acceptable.

The premonition of dread that I felt that fateful morning was right on the mark and later into her pregnancy mother experienced another one of her own. She was well into her forth month when it happened and like the other times it had occurred unexpectedly in the middle of the night when mother awoke to the dreaded sounds of some loud, simultaneous knocks. Sitting up in bed with a start mother feared the worst as the hairs on the back of her neck stood up and an eerie icy chill ran down her spine. She tried to go back to sleep but could not. Father tried questioning her before leaving for work that morning but mother was completely unnerved and didn't want to talk about it.

By the time I woke and went into the kitchen I was surprised to see that she was already up and sitting at the kitchen table staring off into space while cradling her cup of coffee. When I asked what was wrong she told me and said that in the night she'd heard two very loud and distinct noises and that she was bracing herself for what was to come. As she spoke a pair of mourning doves flew over and perched on the kitchen window sill and sat cooing before flying off together which gave us both pause. It was not until that afternoon that we got the call that mother was dreading would come.

The phone rang two longs and a short. It was our ring. When mother picked up the line and heard her sister's voice on the other end bearing the awful news it made mother clutch her stomach, drop to her knees and sob. The sad tidings, brought by Flo, revealed the mystery of the two knocks mother heard in the night. They concerned our beloved Ruby and Warren who had been murdered in their beds. Aunt Flo's voice trembled as she described the grizzly scene at Ruby's house. The evidence was tough to bear as Flo said that Warren was easily recognized but that she'd identified Ruby by a mole they both knew she had on her right thigh. Mother put the phone down and rushed around in a panic throwing some things into her valise before heading out to the depot. The last thing she said was that she'd call us as soon as she got to Florence's.

When father came home that evening he was taken aback by the news and her abrupt departure. Understanding the pressing urgency behind her leaving, a great part of his concern was for their yet to be born babies wellbeing. Thankfully father was at home when the call came in from mom that she had arrived and that she and her sister were going to the crime scene to clean up the mess. Ruby and Warren's bodies had been removed earlier but everything else was undisturbed. The two of them were made to scrub their mingled blood and brains from off of the walls and floor. The unfathomable horror was something no family member should have to face on their own and so father, after asking some friends of his to check in on us, drove north to attend the funerals and support his expecting wife.

The morning dad left the story broke of Ruby and Warren's double homicide. Local papers carried the sorted details of what had taken place that fateful night. It was reported as a crime of passion and that a suspect was in custody. Police were called to the scene by neighbor's who alerted them that they heard shooting in the dark and witnessed a man running from the house. When police arrived they picked up on a blood trail that led detective's strait to a Mr. Ralph Crossman whom they subsequently arrested and charged with the murders. Upon a four and a half hour interrogation Mr. Crossman confessed all and that in his own words, "they had it coming."

In order to repair her marriage Ruby confessed to Warren about the affair and had broken all ties with her lover as promised. Warren forgave Ruby and together they put the tryst behind them but Ralph could not and felt jilted. With Ruby's and Ralph's relationship over, Crossman went to their home armed with a shotgun and seeking revenge for the turmoil he felt she'd caused him. He said that when he got there the pair of them was soundly sleeping until he shot Warren in the back of his head which woke Ruby and had her setting up in bed pleading for her life which was when he shot Ruby at point-blank range in her face.

Reading the article made me to realize just how right mother had been when she warned Ruby that she was playing a dangerous game and I'd wished she would have taken heed but it seemed that once you're an adult your choices are your own, good or bad. I saved the article but never showed it to anyone. While some of my innocence died in the Cork's shed the rest died with my Aunt Ruby, God Bless her soul. Mother and father returned from Indiana after the funerals and life went on. Not much was ever said about Ruby and Warren's untimely demise until it was reported that Ralph Crossman had died in prison of syphilis two years later.

CHAPTER SEVENTEEN
THE SILENCING OF THE LUNCHBOXES

Just after mother went into labor and gave birth to a six pound baby girl she sunk into a great depression. Ironic our lovely Ruby Mae made her debut appearance on Tuesday, October 29th, 1929, also known infamously as Black Tuesday and the start of North Americas Great Depression. There was something else I found incredibly ironic about Ruby Mae's birth and the state of the nation was that when mother first received the news she was with child it was her choice to jump off the shed roof from despair and the very day our dear Ruby Mae took her first breath a number of Stock Market investors leaped to their death by jumping out of skyscraper windows. One fortunate thing was that mother's great depression as bad as it was did not last as long as the countries.

Because mother was still grieving the loss of her murdered sister, mother decided she would name the new baby Ruby Mae in her honor but even that did not help curb the erratic mood-swings that grew more worrisome with each passing day. Mother turned face to the wall and did nothing but sleep for weeks. Because of our growing family and mother's depression father worked as many hours as he could. Evelyn and I tended to Ruby Mae around the clock until mother could cope which was not easy without her help. Everything had changed so much since the baby arrived and my body and moods were not exempt. James was growing and so were my budding breast. As my body changed so did my temperament. At fifteen I felt to be at my wits end and gripped that I needed her help and to my surprise instead of mother snapping at me or dismissing my complaint she came around and took over which was a great relief for us all.

It was on one of those days when mother was feeling better that she insisted her and I sit down for what she called, "The Talk." What I was hearing was embarrassing beyond belief, most of which I already knew. A few months earlier Marcy Donavan had started her menstrual cycle and was keen to tell Evelyn and I all about what sounded to me to be a bloody mess and one that I was not looking forward too. Mother went into a grand dissertation about what it was to be female and that once my period arrived I could expect it every month for the rest of my life. What a rude awakening to womanhood that was. Even more embarrassing was when mother handed me a small package lying beside her in the chair but I had no idea what it was having never seen it before and after clearing her throat held it out to me like it was some kind of a gift.

"What's this?" I asked taking the lightweight package.

"You'll see once you open it," She insisted but even after I opened the box and looked it over I still didn't know what it was or what I was supposed to do with it.

"Ah, come on Rose, it's a sanitary belt and not just any sanitary belt, it's a Hickory" Mom boasted.

"What do I need this for?" I asked puzzled, hoping I was wrong.

"It's for when you start, silly"

"Oh," I said disappointed that it wasn't something I wanted.

Mother grabbed her gift from me and explained that it was the best on the market.

"But Rosie, it's a Hickory, the belt that never binds." She seemed very proud to have bought me the top of the line when it came to sanitary belts.

Then as if my humiliation could not get any worse mom brought out another long thick cotton thing that had long floppy bits on each end. While holding the belt she began weaving the thin long bits through the toothy metal ends to demonstrate how it worked. The Talk was awful and not at all what I was anticipating. It had nothing to do with sex just a lot of nonsense about something that I hoped would never happen to me. The next subject mom brought up was even more horrifying than the first as the topic started with three very troubling words; "Douching with Lysol," I thought I might faint.

Mom explained that once I did start my menstrual cycle I would have to clean myself inside every month and that the only proper way to do that was to douche and that the best douche was Lysol. Her going on made my head spin. That was when our talk was taken into the bathroom where she showed me what I would be using to hold the disinfectant and warm water which would flush out any and all bacteria that built up inside after my monthly cycle ended. I understood that flushing our toilet was good but what she was asking me to flush out sounded disgusting not to mention painful. I'd seen her douche bag and Lysol a hundred times but had never put the two together and had no idea what she did with them. It looked like an implement of torture and from what she was telling me, it was.

By then I had heard enough and after developing a new appreciation for what all of womankind was made to endure I asked if I could lay down and went to bed early that night wishing I was born a boy and praying that I would not have to go into the dark abyss of womanhood any time soon but my pleas went unanswered and must had bounced off the ceiling as it were only a few short weeks after, "our talk," that I needed to strap on the old belt and had a date with our household disinfectant.

And it wasn't just me that was changing everything was as the whole of America sank into a sea of despair. Across the east factories of all sorts closed their doors despite the cost of living spiraling and out of control. Pittsburgh's middle class had all but disappeared and life went from hard, to really tough, to extremely hard, to damn near impossible for us and a great many other people trying to keep food on the table. Everyone needed to tighten their belts in order to survive. We thought ourselves lucky to have some savings in the bank but that was until our bank failed and every cent my father had managed to put away disappeared like snow in a spring thaw and like the floods that come after the thaw the hordes of unemployed flooded the streets aimlessly.

One by one the mills shut down as there gates were padlocked. Duquesne Steel and the rest of the steel mills along the Mon Valley soon faced crippling levels of unemployment. Even the massive mill in Braddock, U.S. Steel, closed. Gone were the deep pockets of the steel companies that funded our libraries, hospital, athletic clubs, and most of the social programs that we depended on. Most of Pennsylvania's mid-sized industrial towns faired the same. Towns like Altoona, Reading, and Johnstown shared a similar fate. Philadelphia, although there were jobs because of the cities diversity, had their own problems. The world went mad causing deadly riots, strikes, marches, lock-outs, bombings and mass demonstrations to erupt in otherwise peaceful towns. Pennsylvanians living on farms and in small rural areas did alright because they could live off the land and weren't dependent upon a weekly check to purchase whatever it was they needed.

The steel mill where father worked had all but shut down, limping along with a skeleton crew while having most of its laborers made redundant, my father included. The evening father came home after work and set his old beat up lunchbox down on our pantry shelf never to be picked up again was a sad day indeed. Each time any one of us was sent to the pantry to collect a tin of food or a jar of something pickled we'd see father's lunchbox sitting there collecting dust and taking up space. The pantry shelf looked larger and larger as the food it once held quickly depleted until dad's rusting lunchbox was the only thing remaining on the shelf. After that there was no need to open the pantry door for food because it was all gone. I never realized how much I enjoyed hearing the joyful sound of those metal lunchboxes clanking together as the hoards of mill employees headed off for work. It was sad to think that those days were gone, but gone they were and my heart broke watching my always happy father loose his way and his ambition.

CHAPTER EIGHTEEN
OKLAHOMA BOUND

Back then standing in long breadlines was not only heart-breaking it was necessary if you wanted something to eat. Hundreds upon hundreds of otherwise able-bodied men stood toe to toe shuffling along in those long lines with a lost look of surrender and hopelessness in their eyes reminiscent of cattle going to the slaughterhouse but in their case the only thing being slaughtered was their pride.

When Ruby Mae turned two years old, mother applied and found work as a cleric downtown. Women weren't paid on the same scale as men but they were paid and what little money she could make was enough to keep us eating, maybe not high off the hog but I am sure hog parts were involved. Tins of spam and thick sliced bologna were our mainstay. Both products made great sandwiches of which we were extremely appreciative. If one of our neighbors was in a tight spot we would take them as much as we could spare. No one was willing to watch the other one starve. We all pitched in and although many of us were hungry most of the time, nobody died because of it.

The depression brought with it government food relief programs where they doled out easy to store items. Such things as powdered milk, dried fruits, margarine, raisins, that could keep us afloat and our stomachs from rubbing against our backbones. The supplies offered may not have been enough to fill our tummies completely but it was enough to stave off the griping pain and we found that every little bit helped. There were no fussy eaters and we were thankful for every scrap we were able to put into our mouths.

Luckily the Evan's clan, of which I belonged, were fighters, both within and without the house. My good friend Jeff Davis's parents were anything but and were of a wimpy nature. The Davis family had barely scrapped by before the depression struck and after it hit Jeff's parents sank into an even deeper state of despair. It seemed that their house had been built on the proverbial sand and when the winds of times hit, their foundation crumbled from underneath them. Jeff's parents lacked gumption and so they lived in squalor for which their son never made excuses for. It was simply how they lived and Jeff adapted without complaint or abandonment. He'd never known anything else and still Jeff had enough intestinal fortitude to never lose his humor or resolute. Jeff had an uncanny knack of peering through the muck without it affecting his character that remained intact. He always amazed me and I was in awe of his strength despite his circumstances which was what I admired about him the most. He, in spite of it all, was longsuffering and because I was not as patient as he. Jeff's very nature helped me keep things in proper prospective. My assumption was that I could always count on Jeff, and he on me and we could until that dreaded morning when Jeff came around to tell me he and his family were moving far away.

At first I thought it was a cruel joke but Jeff was never one to be cruel. It turned out that he had an aunt and uncle in Oklahoma that wanted their assistance and invited them to stay on their farm where they could help plant and harvest the wheat. When I realized he meant it I asked when they would be leaving and he told me they were already packed and ready to go. Because of the hard times, the Davis's had already moved a number of times on account they could not make rent but this move was different, it was out of state and Oklahoma sounded like a foreign country on the other side of the world. For the Davis's it could not have happened at a more opportune time. Jeff said they were about to be evicted again and it would have been anyone's guess where they would have ended up after that if it had not been for their invite to Oklahoma. They would probably have landed in one of the crime ridden shantytowns that were popping up all over Pittsburgh and throughout Pennsylvania which were nothing more than makeshift slums.

Jeff continued talking about all the things that I was not ready to hear. The sound of his voice changed and became a confusing blur that was vaguely recognizable and everything went into a kind of slow motion as I tried calculating how far Oklahoma was from Pittsburgh in my mind. He said he was in a hurry and needed to get back but because I wasn't ready to let him go just yet I walked with him to his place.

As we walked and I started asking questions everything began to sink in.

"How ya gunna get there?" I asked, knowing they didn't have a pot to piss in or a window to throw it out of.

Jeff told me that because his aunt and uncle wanted them out there so badly they had extended them some money and that with the needed funds his father had bargained with a man and had bought a truck and an army tent and that because his father had succored such a good deal they still had a little money for gas and food along the way.

Jeff told me that his aunt and uncle were farmers and that they had planted a bumper crop of wheat and that because the harvest was so big they were running their tractor day and night and really needed the help. It all sounded like a load of rubbish to me and in my opinion, if they expected Jeff's parents to go out there and work the land I thought they were sadly mistaken. Jeff would have been a great asset, but his folks, never. The pair of them was not worth Jeff's spit in my opinion but I would never say it. They had nothing here to hold them and so part of me understood why his father would jump at a chance to make a change and Oklahoma sounded as drastic of a change as they could make.

Jeff said his aunt claimed that growing wheat was the new gold rush and that they should get out there quick and apply to Homestead before all the land was gone. She said that in Oklahoma the government had just upped the acreage available and that they could be granted a square mile parcel of land which equated to 640 workable acres and that if they helped them bring in their big harvest they could pay the Davis's in enough seed to plant their own field which sounded very promising. Jeff said that the minute his father received the letter he was so excited by the prospect of being a landowner that he was like a new man and set his sights on making the arrangements. With no time to waste before the sheriff came to toss them out on their ears again Mr. Davis took the money his sister sent him and bought an old jalopy and an army tent for them to live in until they could build their own place on their own property. Mr. Davis had hope that Oklahoma would be his field of dreams and as soon as he had succored the transportation and a tent for them to live in he felt prepared for the for their new adventure and journey westward.

As Jeff and I approached the latest place the Davis's resided and saw the truck parked out front piled high with everything they owned including the army tent Jeff had told me his father bought I burst into tears. That old jalopy didn't look like it would make it out of town let alone all the way to Oklahoma. Because it all happened so suddenly I wanted to give Jeff something to remember me by but the only thing I could think of was a lock of my hair and so while Jeff was in the house I asked Mrs. Davis if she had some scissors handy and to my surprise she did. With haste I cut off a lock of my hair and braided the cutting. When Jeff wasn't looking I slipped it into his knapsack. Jeff promised again that he would write to me and we swore to each other that as soon as the country bounced back we could find each other and make a life together. My secret hope when I wished upon a star was that one day we would marry and live happily ever after. Jeff and I had never discussed what our long term future would be but it was always a dream of mine.

Once I got my wits about me, I realized we were giving our final farewells and no matter how much we wished we had a future together, it seemed that fate had other plans for us. Looking into his loving eyes I again burst into tears knowing I would probably never see his shining face again. Jeff didn't cry like me but his eyes did well up with tears. Saying goodbye to each other was the hardest thing we had ever done and after a long tearful embrace and all our goodbyes said I watched helplessly as he and his folks climbed aboard their newly acquired truck to leave Pittsburgh for good. It took a few cranks to get the jalopy going and after it jumped and backfired loudly Jeff and I burst onto laughter remembering the time when we'd tried to start my dad's car and all the trouble I'd gotten into for it. Our laughter broke the tension and although it was difficult for me to picture Jeff's parents as land owners let alone farmers I wished them well and stood in the street waving wildly watching their sputtering jalopy disappear from view headed to destinations unknown. It all seemed like a harebrained idea but if it worked out according to plan it would be wonderful for them which gave me hope that if they earned enough money Jeff would send for me.

As soon as I walked in the door my mom asked why I was so down in the mouth and I told her about Jeff and his family and that they had left Pittsburgh for good and were already on their way to Oklahoma. Seeing how upset I was over it my mom allowed me to grieve for the rest of the day but by the next day she didn't want to hear anything about Jeff and even made a snide comment that it was for the best and good-riddance to them. Her response was crushing but I did my best to keep the hurt feelings to myself and went into a deep mourning for my lost love.

While Jeff's leaving was my worst day, my best day came in the form of a letter headed, "My Darling Rose."

In keeping with his promise Jeff had written me and posted it while they were still on the road. Even before they reached their destination Jeff wrote. Excitedly my hands shook nervously as I traced every line with my finger knowing his hand had crossed there. His words made my heart flutter and I kissed the page and then held it to my heart. Jeff had never spoken of romance and now that he was gone forever he'd gained the courage to say what was is his heart all along and I realized that we felt the same about each other.

His letter went on to say that he'd found my lock of hair in his knapsack and that he would treasure it always. Jeff planned on keeping a journal of their farming experiences and that he was looking forward to sharing his thoughts with me. He'd written to me during the second leg of their travels and noted that the night prior they'd slept in their car parked behind a big wooden billboard advertizing an Amoco Gasoline Station in the next town when they were approached by a couple of hobo's in search of food. Jeff said they couldn't spare much but that his father had cut them a bologna and mustard sandwich for them to share before going on their way. Because of the great distance they were traveling Jeff's father was allowing him to share in the driving which he said was great fun because he'd never got the chance to drive our car and that he was looking forward to driving the tractor on his aunt and uncle's farm.

Jeff's letter continued by telling me that while on the road he'd seen a magnificent shooting star and that he thought of me and made the wish that we would be together again. When he revealed what he'd wished for I feared he had jinxed us and worried that we'd never see each other again. Jeff closed the letter promising he would write again soon and that he truly loved me and always would. His tender words overwhelmed me. I must have read his first letter a hundred times but until I knew his address I had no place to send my reply but wrote a lengthy letter to him anyhow and waited. Knowing I would be receiving more letters I asked my father if he could get me a cigar box so I could keep them in.

By the weekend father brought home and gave me an empty cigar box that he'd acquired from one of the many bartenders he knew and liked and after rifling through a bag of fabric scraps that I'd put aside because they were far too pretty to get rid of I began my project and made some paste out of flour, boiling water and a pinch of sugar. After pasting my fancy swatches onto the cigar box I used a scrap of ribbon and made a rosette that I stuck through with a straight pin so I could seal my newly transformed keepsake box. It turned out great and I was very pleased with how it looked. After placing Jeff's letter inside I kept it under my bed so I could pull it out and read it in the night.

While waiting for Jeff's next letter things at home grew more strained. The economy was slipping farther and farther down the drain and so was my father. Because the factories had closed and there was no work to be found I watched as my father became listless and looked sad all the time which wasn't like him. One day a couple of his drinking buddies from the mill stopped by the house and invited to take him out for the day to get his mind off his troubles. It had been the first time I'd seen my dad smile since the plant closed. Together they went off and were gone for hours and hours.

Rather than being happy that dad was able to enjoy a good time for a change mother became furious and took to her room where she sat alone in the darkness. The longer he stayed out the angrier she became until she snapped over her lot in life and slammed their bedroom door shut. Unbeknownst to us, who were relieved that she'd finally gone to bed, she instead started plotting her revenge and after rooting through the closet and pulling out and loading father's shotgun sat in a chair in the dark waiting for him to come home. We all knew mother was really angry that night but we had no idea that she had murder on her mind and a gun in her hand. When father came home that night he was legless and yet when he opened their bedroom door and saw mother pointing his gun sobered him up quickly and he rushed her before she was able to get a shot off. The awful commotion brought all of us running from our room to see what was going on.

Thankfully father had managed to get the gun away from her before it went off. Dad took his gun into the kitchen sat down at the table and removed the cartridges from both chambers and shook his head over what had just happened. Mother's temporary bout with insanity left her crumpled up and lying on their bedroom floor sobbing. It was awful and terrifying and we were all very shaken by the experience. I don't think anyone was able to sleep that night.

The following day when everyone got up we all went about our business as though nothing unusual had happened. We never spoke of that night but afterwards every time I spotted dad staggering up the road towards the house happily singing one of his old Welsh songs I feared mom would snap again. It was difficult to understand why dad pushed her so far but I imagined he had his own torments, mom's endless bouts with depression and her behavior being two of them.

CHAPTER NINETEEN
LETTERS OF HOPE

For me the most anxious part of my day was waiting for the postman. Whenever one of Jeff's letters arrived they were headed the same way. "My Darling Rose." Those three little words were like music to my ears and meant the world to me. The distance seemed to give him a freedom to express his true feelings towards me in ways he'd never done before. Realizing how he felt made me long to be with him even more.

Jeff wrote that after over eight days on the road they'd arrived safely and that his aunt and uncle were thrilled to bits to see them. After a grand reunion they partook in a virtual feast to celebrate the event. Because the sun had already set by the time they pulled up to the farm Jeff's aunt and uncle insisted they stay in the house for the night. Early the next morning they set up camp in the yard. Jeff said that when they first pitched their tent it had not been packed properly and that the canvas smelt of mold but that because there was a good stiff breeze and not a cloud in the sky he expected the odor would clear out quickly.

Jeff's words drew a picture in my mind as he described Oklahoma. He wrote that the farm was a vast field of golden wheat with clear blue skies. Jeff said and that his aunt's and uncle's house was left unfinished but that it was in better shape than they were used to. They'd pitched their tent behind the house which helped block some of the wind and that there were a couple of outbuildings in the yard near the house and a corncrib to store animal feed. They had a small chicken coop stocked with a few hens and a rooster that not only crowed at the break of dawn but whenever he had a mind to. They kept two cows but no bulls and he wrote that his aunt and uncle had an indoor toilet but that, like when they were living in Pittsburgh, was not yet hooked and so it was back to the outhouse for them all. His aunt Opal had promised that the bathroom was the very next project on their, to do, list and that as soon as they got the money from their soon to be harvested wheat they would finish it. He said that his aunt was a wonderful cook and that everything she made was fresh and good that she and her husband were hardworking no nonsense kind of people which made me wonder how they and Jeff's folk's would get along.

His letters made for marvelous reading and although I could picture him driving that tractor he wrote about I had a hard time picturing his parents putting their hands to the plough. Jeff said that he drove his uncle Earl's tractor through the night when everyone else was asleep and that the tractor was equipped with large overhead lights so he could see and that he enjoyed the solitude of driving through the night. To picture him bouncing along on the springy seat steering the tractor, singing the night away put a smile on my face. He wrote that while driving the tractor he felt closer to me and that the magnificent sunrises and sunsets from atop the tractor were his favorite times of the day and that he loved Oklahoma claiming there was like no other place on earth like it and that the only thing missing in his newly found paradise was me. Jeff said his aunt and uncle had wild turkeys that they were caring for and that their farm stretched over a mile and that the wheat crop was already waist high and ready to be harvested. He said there were no trees or hills, just rolling grasslands and beautiful skies for as far as you could see. Jeff admitted that the work was hard but confessed he enjoyed it immensely and claimed that they'd accomplished a great deal since he'd arrived.

They might have been living like nomads but it all sounded so picturesque and a kind of heaven on earth and a perfect utopia with food galore and wide open spaces. It calmed me and I felt secure knowing that Jeff was safe and happy and thought that nothing could spoil what he'd found. After receiving a few of his letters I'd gone to our local library where I searched through a map of Oklahoma so I could see the area where Jeff was living. It was difficult to find at first because it was obscurely located smack dab in the middle of a narrow strip of land that jetted out above the Texas panhandle. Where he was, bordered Kansas and Colorado and the county where they lived in was in fact called Texas County, Oklahoma.

In a different letter Jeff wrote that the sheer beauty of the landscape was so different than Pittsburgh he had not realized such beauty existed outside of my eyes which was amazing to read and made my heart skip a beat. He'd become so poetic in his writings I'd wished I could share his letters with the world but they were meant just for me and I cherished every one of them.

Jeff compared the gentle winds sweeping over the prairie bending the willowy stalks of wheat to a graceful dancer dipping his partner at the end of a song. Jeff had a way of making everything sound so splendid I could not wait to join him and had already begun putting away money with that intent. I'd earned a little bit mending neighbors clothes and what I didn't give to my parents to help make ends meet I stowed away alongside Jeff's letters in my handy keepsake box under my bed. Jeff would have been proud of me as I had become quite the seamstress.

His grand letters gave me hope and with every correspondence my mood and ambition was raised to new heights. Because his letters were so uplifting I only wanted to write about the good things so I could encourage him as much as he was encouraging me but sometimes good news was hard to find.

Because of the Depression everything in and around Pittsburgh was getting tight including Ruby Mae's and James shoes. Evelyn and I were lucky in that our feet had stopped growing and we weren't as hard on the leather soles as they were. Ruby Mae didn't need much as far as clothing because we could sew but poor James was growing like the wheat Jeff described and was in need of everything.

The Hobo's that had taken to the rails seemed freer than us. Although times were hard they were in some ways the best of times as well. Everyone was feeling the pinch including the once wealthy class. We at least had neighbors and friends we could count on but the rich, once their money was gone, had nothing. Our neighbors helped one another in ways they had never done before. If we had an extra potato or carrot we shared it and our neighbors did the same. It was humbling and invigorating at the same time and built a kind of character in us that could not be torn down or matched.

The churches and private charities like the Salvation Army were doing all they could to keep everyone afloat but our sea of despair was deepening and at times felt like it would swallow us alive. The crisis the eastern part of the country was going through had grown so fast it was impossible to keep up with the needs of the hungry and at no other time in American history were so many people struggling to survive and my family was no exception.

Jeff got some news about the struggles in the east from newsreels that he saw at his town center. Jeff said everyone in Oklahoma thought that the problem facing the country was more of an eastern phenomenon and would never impact them in the same way it did us. I could tell he was growing concerned about my welfare and so I wrote to assure him that everything was fine and good except for missing him.

Government officials put out informative newsreels claiming the rain followed the plough encouraging homesteaders to plant as much as they could to feed the world. Thus the plain states were labeled the breadbasket of the world. In the newsreels they depicted farmer after farmer harvesting vast quantities of ripened wheat and I pictured my Jeff on one of those tractors coming to our rescue bringing the food we desperately needed with him.

As soon as the spring crop was brought in and they had a bit of money Jeff's father filed for their homestead status which he gained and so they would be moving yet again. The profit in planting wheat was theirs for the taking and even if the price continued to drop some it was still worth doing. That first harvest that they helped with was a real bonanza and according to Jeff's aunt and uncle it was the biggest crop by far that anyone in them parts had ever seen. The plain states farmers were next year people in that they hoped that the next year would be even more prosperous than the last and for their sakes I had the same hope for them. Jeff explained why wheat was the crop to go with because it could be planted and harvested twice a year doubling their profit while fully utilizing the land.

From where we were and they were it appeared that the Davis's had made the right decision to move when they did. Leaving Pittsburgh and going to Oklahoma gave me hope that Jeff had escaped, what to us seemed like, the destruction of mankind but no matter how hungry or worn my clothes were it always brought a smile to my face imagining Jeff happily perched atop his uncle's tractor driving over the vast countryside under a clear starlight night and I knew that every time he'd see a shooting star he'd make another wish for us to be together more than quadrupling our chances.

CHAPTER TWENTY
THE DIRTY THIRTIES

That first year of Jeff moving west was hard on both of us. He was so busy trying to make a go at farming that his letter writing suffered. While Jeff and his family struggled to plough and plant their newly acquired acreage a terrible drought began to strangle the plain states farmers and Oklahoma turned out to be the epicenter for the longest dry spell in American history. When Jeff lived with his aunt and uncle he wrote faithfully but those days were gone and they were now living in an area of Oklahoma called Boise. Initially Jeff sounded very excited about starting anew and felt confident that their farm would be as great of a success as his aunt and uncles was. Bolstering his confidence was the fact that the last crop they helped bring in was the largest his Aunt Opal and Uncle Earl had ever seen. The glut from the season's bumper crop caused the price of wheat to plunge and so for a wage, Jeff and his family were paid in seed. Enough to plant the entire estimated sixty acres they'd acquired through homesteading. Besides the seed Opal and Earl threw in a couple of turkey chicks as a bonus and what money they could spare after finishing their bathroom.

After purchasing some lumber the Davis's erected a make-shift cabin for them to live in. To make things stretch they, like us, left nothing go to waste. Their old tent was cut up and used to help insulate the cabin roof and walls and the rest of it was used to shelter the turkeys after installing a fenced in an area in the yard. Jeff's aunt and uncle had warned them that turkeys were the stupidest of all birds and that if they did not have a roof over their heads when it rained they'd look up and drown. Jeff wrote that it was hard but fulfilling work and that they had accomplished a lot in a few short months. Correspondence was our lifeline but like the drought affecting the land our letters were drying up too. Neither of us wanted to be responsible for discouraging the other and with times getting harder for everyone there didn't seem to be much else to write about.

Working sixty acres of land was probably more than they could manage and I couldn't help but worry. Their farm was isolated and over fifty miles away from Opal and Earl's place. The work sounded demanding and even Jeff admitted that there were no shortcuts in farming. For need of a tractor the Davis's started their farm deep in debt after borrowing the money against their first crop that didn't come in. As farmers the Davis's were greener than the sprouting wheat they first planted. They were city folks that just so happened to work on a family farm for a short season making their latest exploit foolhardy at best.

Those first few encouraging crops that the Davis's helped bring in while living at their aunt and uncle's farm turned out to be the beginning of the end for not only them but for all the plain state farmers. With no time to cry over the collapsing prices Opal and Earl went back to the plough as Jeff and his family attempted to do the same on their plot of land. Because Opal and Earl had worked the farm for most of their lives they were well aware of just how obstinate the weather in them parts could be. It took a great deal of grit and stamina to endure the strong blustery winds and the earth cracking droughts that nature threw at them over the years and true grit was something Jeff's folks lacked.

When the drought started, America's Agricultural Department made claim that, "rain followed the plough," and doled out the huge 640 acre parcels to anyone willing to homestead and cultivate the land. Encouraged by the government's claim, novice homesteaders, the Davis's included, rushed to the till and plowed massive swatches of acreage scarring the land that exacerbated an already tenuous situation. The government sponsored champagne for planting continued long after the worst drought in American history had crippled the country.

The once prosperous American Plains that had been labeled the breadbasket of the world before the great plough up had fallen prey to the drought. The constant displacement of the lands fragile topsoil unbalanced the entire eco system in unprecedented ways creating a more adverse effect than anyone could have imagined. The promise of wealth for the farmers had all but disappeared. Gone were the gray rolling clouds that brought moister and abundant life to the grasslands. Without the precious rainfall, crop after crop failed and carried on failing season after disappointing season. The long drought brought even the seasoned farmers to their knees with heartfelt prayers on their lips and sand sifting through their fingers. The harsh reality of little to no rain continued on month after month and year after year.

Things became so bad for the farmers they made up catchy songs; "It ain't gonna rain no more, no more, it ain't gonna rain no more; How in the heck can I wash my neck if it ain't gonna rain no more!"

The struggle continued and farmers tightened their belts as the land dried up around them and blew away. With all of nature working against them they found themselves stuck in the doldrums with little hope of coming through on the other side. They did everything they could to save their merger crops and when the coyotes came in and threatened their livestock they had no choice but to eradicate them. With no coyotes feeding on the ever multiplying jackrabbits the very crops the farmers wanted to protect was put in jeopardy. The unmanageable starving jackrabbit population descended upon them by the thousands and devoured their budding spring wheat before they could be stopped. To kill the jackrabbits, farmers amassed great hunts and went out with clubs, shovels, rakes and guns.

One of the last letters I'd received from Jeff spoke of how sorry he was about killing those poor rabbits. It seemed all the news coming out of Oklahoma was dire and out of control. Reports had it that there were impenetrable clouds of red, yellow, or brown gritty dust swirling across the five states and that they blew in without warning. The color of the so called "dusters" depended on the color of the displaced topsoil from where the storm originated. Without topsoil and rain seeds could not germinate and lay stagnant transforming the land into miles and miles of virtual desert and was quickly becoming uninhabitable.

Without the cooling rain, temperatures soared leaving the ground so parched it cracked from the heat. Furnace like winds churned temperatures in excess of 118 degrees and rolled aimlessly over the plains. News Week Magazine dubbed the Great Plains, "A vast simmering Cauldron," and a virtual, "Hell on Earth," and I worried how Jeff would survive.

The blistering temperatures stunted the stalks of corn the farmer had planted to feed their hungry animals. It had become so miserably hot that the malnourished ears of corn literally baked in their husks and were not fit for even animal consumption. The next curse that hit the beleaguered farmer was of biblical proportion when grasshoppers too numerous to count descended upon their fields. Thick black clouds of them so large in size they could block the noonday sun from shining. Winged insects that packed such a veracious appetite they devoured everything in their path and when they ran out of wheat and corn to eat they took to the trees and began devouring the bark. Desperation made the farmers take to the combines in an attempt to harvest their meager crops before the grasshoppers got it all but their numbers were so great they clogged the blades on the combines from turning and stopped them in their tracks.

Throughout the Great Plain States the banks began foreclosing on properties causing many a farmer to go bust which spurred a great migration west to California. The little bit of money the banks did bring in was not enough to save them and they too failed just as the banks had in the east. With desperate times come desperate measures and the agony of the day gave birth to the desperadoes. People like Pretty Boy Floyd, Machine Gun Kelly, John Dillinger, Bonnie and Clyde came roaring onto the scene robbing banks. Because they had started off as everyday folk Pretty Boy Floyd and John Dillinger gained a great deal of notoriety and support from the common folk.

John Dillinger had started his life of crime as a teenager when he was jailed for an attempted robbery. While in jail John learned from his fellow inmates the tricks of the trade and after being a model prisoner was paroled in 1933. With connections gained in jail Dillinger amassed a group of likeminded thugs and he and his gang embarked on a yearlong crime spree that enthralled the nation and eluded police. One of Dillinger's gang was dubbed Baby Face Nelson after a youthful picture of him appeared in the paper. Because he was able to escape capture for so long, John Dillinger made it to the top of J. Edgar Hoover's public enemy number one list and it wasn't until, "the lady in red," ambush, where he was gunned down by the Fed's coming out of a Chicago Theater. After that Baby Face Nelson took the title and the mystique surrounding the depression era gangsters continued.

It was not long before Baby Face Nelson met with the same fate as his cohort, Dillinger and was killed by the Fed's in a shootout. Bonnie and Clyde murdered and robbed banks and were notorious for grabbing some of the more scintillating headlines of the day. The ill-fated young lover's were ambushed while driving a stolen car in a hail of gunfire near the Texas-Louisiana boarder. The autopsy reports had Clyde Barrow shot twenty-five times while Bonnie Parker was hit with twenty-three bullets. Over 40,000 people attended Clyde Barrow's funeral while Miss. Bonnie Parker drew a crowd of over 50,000 to hers.

With the terrible poverty stretching across the America's none had it worse than the plains states farmers and the mass exodus of starving vagrants had begun to move west in search of a better life. Unable to survive the frightful dusters that had only intensified over the years much of the livestock choked and lay dead in the fields. One desperate farmer that had become so distraught over his bleating sheep that he counted his losses and slit the throats of his entire herd before tossing their bleeding carcasses over the canyon rather than watch them starve. The massive dust storms were called names like "Black Blizzards" or "Black Rollers." Routinely they kicked up without warning and some were so large they could impact people living thousands of miles away. Without the rain there was only death and starvation as the "Dirty Thirties" gripped America's plains.

It seemed as though the whole of America was heading for hell in a hand basket. Between the stock-market crash of the east and the dust bowl in the west people were pinching pennies so hard Lincoln cried copper tears. A man once said that when America sneezed the whole world caught the cold but for most Americans living in the Thirties were convinced that their cold felt more like a terminal case of pneumonia. The decadent excess of the "Roaring Twenties," were only a fond memory as the trials and tribulations of the decade long "Dust Bowl and the Dirty Thirties" drug on with no end in sight.

With all the strife and hardships engulfing the whole nation it was no wonder that Jeff had stopped writing. Our correspondence had dried up tighter than a popcorn fart and although I kept up the good fight for a time and continued writing it was discouraging when no word came back and so after a few months we lost touch and I moved on in search of other interests to occupy my mind.

CHAPTER TWENTY-ONE
HEADLINES

One of the first stories I followed with fervor covered the American teen culture and the racial tensions in the south. Pittsburgh had its fair share of ethnic unrest but there was no comparison to what the nine jailed Negro youths in Scottsboro Alabama were facing. Their story was the catalysis that brought inequality to the forefront. Because the young men jailed were about my age their story impacted me in ways difficult to express. During the spring of 1931 a group of white teens hopped a freight train which was pretty common place. The boxcar they chose to jump into was otherwise occupied and a fight ensued for control of the space. The teens that were there first, held their ground, tossing the intruding teens back off of the train and because they were Negroes and the other boys tossed from the train were white they were offended and went to the local authorities to report what they believed was a crime. Prejudice ran amuck in the south and so because of that the local police were all too eager to get involved.

The train was stopped and a witch-hunt ensued. One by one the cars were searched until the posse found and promptly arrested nine Negro youths they discovered hunkered down in one of the boxcars. At the time of their arrest the young men were accompanied by two transient white girls traveling with them. Because the girls were white the police refused to accept the fact they were there on their own accord and took them for intense questioning. To explain their predicament the girls made claim that they'd been raped and feared for their lives. The girl's statements then matched the sheriff's preconceived belief and so they were released but the boys were not so lucky. Punishment for such serious allegations was death by hanging. The nine youths awaiting trial ranged in age from sixteen to twenty and because of the notoriety of the case Scottsboro was inundated with reporters as their trial commenced.

The officials of Scottsboro did not appreciate all the scrutiny brought on by the press and so to get the spotlight off their town pushed for a speedy trail. The southern states had their own form of handling judicial matters and race relations and had no intentions of allowing the northern sympathizers to judge how they ran things.

Recognizing Scottsboro's intent, a campaign was organized to write letters of outrage which were sent to the courthouse in protest. A great many people were demanding that, Scottsboro Police release and pardon all nine young men citing the charges were drummed up and bogus. The great divide between northerners and southerners grew to new proportions and was palpable. Likeminded citizens across the land were horrified by the travesty of justice being carried out in Scottsboro and feared that the trial was just another avenue for Alabama to hold a legal lynching.

The Scottsboro Boys trial only lasted a few weeks and as expected all but the youngest boy was sentenced to death. While awaiting appeal Ministers preached sermons about the youth's plight. Albert Einstein and other men of renown spoke in their defense. Jazz artist like Cab Calloway and Duke Ellington conducted benefits to help raise legal funds and awareness. While Welsh poet, L. Hughes visited the nine in the penitentiary he was moved to pen words concerning, "Brown America," being locked up unjustly. The case was brought before America's Supreme Court and was overturned but because of the tenacity of the southern lawyers their original findings were eventually substantiated and subsequently they able to conduct a new trial all the while, the nine teens languished in prison making the Supreme Court's ruling into a hollow victory at best.

While awaiting their next trial another even more sensational story gripped the country taking the spotlight off of Scottsboro and moving it over to the breaking news coming out of New Jersey when America's darling aviator, Charles Lindbergh and his only heir Charles Jr. was stolen in the night.

It had been a long hard cold winter when the report came in that the world famous pilot's son had been kidnapped. Hordes of reporters converged and released the unbelivable headlines that varied from paper to paper. "CRIB WAS EMPTY - SOBS BETTY" and "ANNE, THEY'VE STOLEN OUR BABY SAID LINDY." Young Charles Jr. was pictured with the caption, "HAVE YOU SEEN THIS BABY?" The Lindbergh baby had the face of an angle from his dimpled chin to his crown of curly blonde hair and gorgeous eyes that appeared to be pleading with the reader for their help. The nurse attending to the boy was the first to discover the empty crib, the open nursery window and the scribbled ransom note that was left behind. The ransom demanded $50,000.00 to be paid and the money drop was arranged after the police were called in.

The unfortunate publicity was a true burden for the Lindbergh's whose only desire was the safe return of their beloved son. Because it was such a high profile of the case, J. Edgar Hoover and his FBI lobbied to change the law making the offence of kidnapping a federal crime punishable by death. When the money drop took place the dollar bills were marked and carefully tracked. It did not take long before Bruno Richard Haupmann, a German immigrant, pulled into a gas station and used one of those traceable bills to purchase petrol for his car. Conscientiously the attendant working recognized what he had and without letting on wrote down Haupmann's license plate number as he drove away. The attendant then went inside and immediately called police and turned over evidence. A dragnet was set capturing the unsuspecting Bruno Richard Haupmann who denied the charge. While Mr. Haupmann went to trial a shallow grave with the decomposing body of a young boy was discovered not far from the Lindbergh's home. The horrible news devastated the country and it was dubbed "The crime of the century."

Newspapers vied against each other to make deadlines as a sea of reporters crammed inside the narrow pews of the courthouse. Outside the courthouse hordes of spectators gathered on the lawn in order to get a glimpse and shout out words of encouragement to the Lindbergh's as they made their way through the madding crowd to attend the trial.

The case was shrouded in mystery and remained in the headlines until well after the conviction was won and Bruno Richard Haupmann, despite his insistence of innocence, was sentenced to death in the electric chair for the kidnapping of the Lindbergh baby. Whether he acted alone or not was anyone's guess but nobody else was ever charged with the crime. Haupmann's conviction gave the world its pound of flesh but in the process America had lost a part of its innocence. After the Lindbergh trial the distinctions between hero's and thugs, good verses' evil grew blurry in the eye of the media who glamorized the gangsters and portrayed the police and FBI as bumbling idiots who couldn't shoot their way out of a paper bag. Movies stared tough actors with attitude like James Cagney who came on the screen driving their big fancy cars wearing the finest of clothes and always had scads beautiful women around them. The movies were big hits with the public and created a distraction from the misery of the day.

CHAPTER TWENTY-TWO
HITCH YOUR CHARIOT TO A STAR

It had been well over three years since I'd received a single word from Oklahoma and by then there was a new aviator to come onto the scene. Amelia Earhart was my hero and my heart soared with hers as she made her solo flight across the Atlantic. Her favorite saying for womankind was, "Hitch your chariot to a star," it felt as though she was talking directly to me and I adored her. Amelia had and independent spirit that could not be quenched and because I wanted to be just like her I cut my hair short in her honor.

While Amelia Earhart was my hero there was a local man by the name of Samuel H. Church who was my father's. The drinking populace of Pittsburgh believed that as long as there was at least one saloon around that kept beer on tap so a thirsty man could drown his sorrows in it, life was at least bearable but without that, all hope was gone and all they had was their own bitter tears to fill their empty glasses. By Ruby Mae's sixth birthday prohibition had taken a real stranglehold on Pittsburgh and my father was missing his drink something terrible. The only ray of hope any of them had was found it the new movement organized by Samuel H. Church, president of the

Carnegie Institute. Mr. Church's valiant efforts to break the back of the existing prohibition laws were, in my father's eyes, heroic. While father might have followed that man to hell and back, my mother wished they would both go there.

President Herbert Hoover had greatly underestimated the power of the nation's financial depression and dust bowl. At the beginning President Hoover infamously declared that the United States had, passed the worst of it and argued that the economy would soon sort itself out without government intervention. The worst, however, had only just begun. President Hoover believed that the federal government should not offer relief to his impoverished country that was becoming dependent upon the breadlines to eat.

Russia's socialistic beliefs left their country practically unaffected by America's Great Depression but that was not the case elsewhere. Every other country around the world shared in our suffering and together we sank into a debilitating sea of despair and hardship that was palpable globally.

Because of President Hoover's apathy his name was stuck on everything lacking. When a man turned his pockets inside out to prove that he had no cash the act was called waving a "Hoover flag." The economic times caused otherwise viable families to move into decrepit shantytowns that because of evictions and foreclosures were springing up all across the country. These shantytowns were mockingly called, "Hooverville's." When a man visited a soup kitchen to get a meal he was ladled out a bowl of what people called, "Hoover Stew." The ever growing homeless population that resorted to using park benches for their beds would cover themselves with old newspapers for warmth and the newspapers were then labeled "Hoover Blanket's."

The passage of time away from Jeff had broken my heart but by my seventeenth birthday I felt I was ready to move on with my life. There was a certain young man that had caught my eye and I his. We saw each other while Evelyn, James and I walked along the railroad tracks picking up coal that fell from passing trains. Collecting the coal was an everyday ritual for us. We needed those scraps of coal to heat our house during those long cold winter months. It made me feel good to do my part as our small contribution was well worth the effort.

School had become expendable for both Evelyn and I but James was still attending. Another way Evelyn and I found we could contribute was to take in mending and ironing. It did not take long before we were good at it and had developed a reputation as capable seamstresses and could mend anything for a minimal fee.

With all the women of the house working and earning a bit of money father became disheartened. It was difficult for him to stand aside an allow us to be the family's breadwinner. For father taking money from the kitty went against his nature but with all the extra time on his hands he began listening to the rhetoric of another local visionary whose name was Father James Cox and although Father Cox was a Catholic priest, his goal was not only for the eternal salvation of one's soul but his goal was to help put an end to the sufferings of the common man.

Our father first met Father Cox while standing in one of his soup lines for a bowl of "Hoover Stew." The always compassionate Father Cox spoke to the growing crowd about his desire to elevate the downtrodden that came to his church day after day for food. He expressed to them that he understood their pain and that their pride might have been bruised but that it was only temporary as long as they united. Father Cox appreciated that the men needed a job and not just another handout and so he started passing around a petition for them to sign. After gathering over six thousand signatures Farther Cox organized a march on Washington DC with the intention of sticking their petition into the president's hand. Because it was such a worthy cause and with so many men out of work the participants gathered and began their march on Washington. Their cause gained momentum and the whole idea snowballed as the protesters wove their way from town to town on their trek to DC.

Father Cox was a former steelworker himself and acting pastorate of the Old St. Patrick's Catholic Church in Pittsburgh. He bore an unwavering conviction to appease the need engulfing the Common Wealth of Pennsylvania. With the added support of the Governor of Pennsylvania who so happened to be a bitter foe of President Hoover, Gifford Pinchot, greeted the oncoming protesters in Harrisburg where even more demonstrators joined the march to the Capital. By the time they reached Washington a formidable army was amassed. The police were called in to manage the crowds but they found them so orderly that the increased patrols were canceled. Instead volunteers came out too set up impromptu field kitchens to feed the weary marchers.

By the time Father Cox, my father and the rest of the protesters arrived the movement had grown from the initial six thousand to over ten thousand strong. It was by far the largest protest Washington had ever seen. President Hoover had initially intended on ignoring their protest and began investigating Father Cox as a radical subversive. The President met with a handful of the protesters and gave them less than a half hour to present their case. Father Cox presented his petition urging the President to provide work and petitioned Congressmen to vote their conscience to provide immediate relief. In a statement to President Hoover, Cox declared "We are not Red demonstrators. We are real honest American citizens and the people I represent here, as well as millions of others throughout the country, are entitled to work. In a country bursting with wealth there is no reason why employment and other relief should not be provided."

When people began asking the marchers how they could afford the trip to Washington they explained they couldn't and that they were not sure if they would be able to make it back. Andrew Mellon, Treasury Secretary, sympathized with their argument and supported the march. Mellon, who owned Gulf Oil Company, quickly ordered his gas stations to dispense gasoline to any of the marchers free of charge. Mellon then learned that hundreds of the men had missed the caravan completely and went into his own pocket covering their train fares. Upon their return to Pittsburgh the "hunger marchers" were welcomed home and provided with a hardy meal in Bohemian Hall. They then held a large rally at Pitt Stadium where Father Cox offered himself as the new Jobless Party's presidential candidate.

The marcher's political impact was dramatic. Treasury Secretary Mellon and President Herbert Hoover had a huge falling out because of it and stopped speaking. Mellon resigned his post and was reappointed ambassador to the UK. With more than 37 percent of the population unemployed the coffers were quickly emptied which ravaged the Commonwealths relief programs. It was a demoralizing state of affairs for Pennsylvania which had prided itself as the workshop of the world. The years that followed produced hordes of dispossessed and the breadlines grew longer. The huddled masses were barely surviving and the makeshift "Hooverville's," were busting at the seams. Pennsylvania carried the burden of the largest number of families seeking relief in the country. Over 324,000 needed some kind of assistance to survive.

The Pittsburgh diocese helped Father Cox establish "Houses of Hospitality" in ethnic, working-class neighborhoods to distribute food and clothing to the multitude of unemployed. There were a number of other local charities that did their best to keep malnutrition and homelessness at bay.

CHAPTER TWENTY-THREE
COMING OF AGE

Turning seventeen brought with it a new range of conflict between me and my mother. While she often pointed out that I was too much like my father I was having difficulty accepting just how mean and spiteful she'd become towards both me and my father. It seemed at times there was no pleasing her despite the fact I willingly contributed financially.

Because I was receiving some positive attention from a certain young man that I only knew as Harold, things seemed to be looking up. Teen boys were seldom employed but Harold was different than most the other boys I knew. They were lucky to land a position as a soda jerk or a paper delivery boy, neither of which paid very much. Companies frowned upon hiring teens in favor of employing men who had families to support. Harold was the exception to the rule and had a real job as a gas station attendant at the nearby Amoco Station where my father faithfully took his car. Harold looked so handsome in his black patent leather brimmed cap and neatly pressed button down shirt with his name proudly embossed over his breast pocket.

We'd noticed each other some months earlier while I collected coal near the railroad tracks. The first time he flirted with me was while he was washing our windshield. That was when he gave me a little wink and a smile. From then on whenever dad needed the car serviced I would ask to go with him. Harold would practically trip over his own legs racing to get to our car.

"What can I do for you today Mr. Evans?" Harold would say while sneaking a flirtatious wink my way which always made me blush.

As the gasoline pumped into the tank Harold would fly into action whipping out his handy oilcloth from his back trouser pocket. After hoisting the hood of our car and removing the radiator cap he'd peek to see if it needed topping up. Then his routine was to check the brake fluid, oil and tire pressure. Harold reminded me of a grand musketeer with our oil stick as his epee. Looking suave Harold pirouetted from around the hood to father's side of the car where he presented him with the oil dip-stick for inspection and possible knighthood which I would have certainly granted.

Harold took particular attention to washing our cars windscreen making sure it was spotless and bug gut free. Father noticed Harold's extra attention to detail and his flirtatious grin as he scrubbed my side of the window and commented that he thought the young man was sweet on me which made me very happy indeed. Flattered by all the attention I began volunteering to run errands so I could go to the Amoco station in hopes of catching a glimpse of him. Sometimes I used the excuse that Ruby Mae needed air in her bicycle tires or sometimes my excuse would be to run up and buy their cigarettes. Most times I took Ruby Mae with me and would treat her to a bottle of coca cola and insisted that she drink every drop while there. Ruby Mae was always happy with the nickels worth of soft drink and I was satisfied with an eyeful of Harold.

One day while Ruby Mae and I were hanging around up at the Amoco station I noticed that Harold's boss was on the premises looking annoyed. Not wanting to get Harold into trouble and while Ruby Mae drank her soda I pushed her bicycle over to the air pump and grabbed the hose. While paying more attention to what Harold and his boss were up to I accidently blew the rear tires tube. The noise scared both me and Ruby Mae who let out a shout of surprise when it popped. Harold's boss looked over at me like I was a blithering idiot. It was so embarrassing I wished the ground could have swallowed me on the spot and I hoped that Harold didn't think me stupid.

Because Ruby Mae's bicycle was now disabled Harold interceded on my behalf asked if he could patch the tube. His boss agreed with the provision Harold put the paying customers first. By the time Harold finished with the tire he'd gathered enough nerve to ask me out on a date providing my father granted permission. I was so excited and scared at the same time. The prospect of going out on a proper date was a little frightening and I worried how my folks would behave when Harold came by our house and prayed they would not be arguing.

My second panic was the thought of what I should wear. Daydreaming about it made me a bundle of nerves as I walked home with Ruby Mae riding her bike in front of me. She'd promised she wouldn't say anything about Harold asking me out but accidently let the news slip as soon as we walked in the door. Worried what our mother would say about me dating I was pleasantly surprised when she appeared excited and even helpful. Encouraged I'd found a young man mother helped me pick out a dress. With a few minor alterations I was able to update the dress to make my outfit more stylish.

The night Harold was to arrive I was in a tizzy and anxious about having a proper date. To prepare I'd read an article in Vogue that dealt with what I might expect while on a date. The article seemed racy and made me wonder if Harold would try to kiss me and if I should allow him to if he did try. The piece covered something they referred to as "French kissing" which sounded so risqué it got my attention right away and so I started practicing by kissing my mirror imagining how it might feel. While Evelyn helped me with my hair we talked about how we thought the night might go. Evelyn seemed as excited as me and because it was such a special occasion mother surprised me and brought out a strand of pearls that she had inherited from her sister Ruby. Those pearls were our mother's most valued possession and it shocked me that she entrusted them into my care and I swore that I would guard them with my life, which was probably what it would have cost me if something bad had happened to them. The pressure to keep them safe almost made me want to decline wearing them at all if it were not for the fact they looked beautiful.

Evelyn and I were still in the bedroom putting some finishing touches on my ensemble when the doorbell rang causing me to nearly jump out of my skin. Mother had already instructed me to stay in my room for a few minutes so I could make a grand entrance. Father wanted to talk to Harold before we left to go out anyhow. When I came out of my room I found Harold standing near the sofa with a small bouquet of flowers in his hand and a broad grin on his face. Father might not have been keen on the idea of me dating but he had already promised me that he would allow it. Father seemed especially worried when he saw that Harold owned his own car. It was rumored that cars in the hands of young men were nothing more than bedrooms on wheels. Before Harold offered me the bouquet he took out a single flower and offered it to my mother who smiled widely and curtseyed at his charming gesture. Mother and I took the rest of the flowers into the kitchen where I snipped the ends before placing them into a vase for everyone to enjoy. They were beautiful and I hated to leave them but was very anxious to see what Harold had in store for us.

After what seemed like an eternity my father's inquisition into Harold's intentions ended and we were allowed to leave. Harold walked me out and came to the passenger side of the car and politely opened the door for me. As we drove away and my date began I waved at Ruby Mae who was standing at the screen door watching us leave.

It seemed strange to be sitting next to Harold. The butterflies moving around in my stomach made me fear I might throw-up. I'd never been alone in a car with anyone except my father before. Harold had promised my mother and father that we were going to see a movie which sounded fine because I loved the movies. When we got to the theater and Harold parked the car I instinctively sat still until he came around and opened the door for me.

The movie was a swashbuckling film called *Mutiny on the Bounty*, that stared Charles Laughton and Clark Gable and we both loved it. We didn't hold hands during the film but Harold did put his arm around my shoulders which made me feel special and cared for. While the movie was running my stomach rumbled which might have been the reason Harold suggested that we go get something to eat afterwards.

There was a diner opened late that he knew about and so we went there. It was bright and clean and almost empty but there were a couple of men sitting at the counter drinking coffee and eating a slice of pie. Harold led me over to the far wall where we sat in a corner booth and looked at the menu. Because I felt a little guilty about all the money Harold had already spent getting the flowers and theater tickets it was a relief when he took the initiative and ordered for the two of us. It was perfect and he ordered exactly what I was hungering for which was a cheeseburger and fries. For our drinks he ordered strawberry milkshakes. It sounded terrific and a heck of a lot better than the tin of spam my folks were probably sharing back at the house.

It was a magical evening and our conversation flowed without the uncomfortable gaffes I'd worried might happen. I even got through my meal without making a mess of my dress and was careful not to speak with a mouthful of food. Harold was doing most of the talking which was fine with me.

When Harold drove me home he asked if it would be alright that he call on me again, to which I eagerly agreed. Our next date was set for the following Saturday evening. As he walked me to the door the palms of my hands began to sweat and I'd wished I brought my gloves. Those few steps to my front door were the scariest of the night and I wondered if he would kiss me or not. My heart was pounding so hard I was having trouble breathing.

The fears that our heads would bump together or worse yet that the onion I'd just eaten on my cheeseburger would be on my breath made French kissing out of the question. We'd just stepped up onto the stoop when someone from inside my house turned on the front porch light abruptly ending our evening allowing me to go inside un-kissed but anxious to see him again. The next time I made a promise to myself that I would ask the waitress to hold the onions.

For me the date went really well and I had a feeling that Harold enjoyed himself too. My mother also appeared excited that Harold had asked me out for a second date. I think she was counting the days before we would be making an announcement of betrothal so I would be out of the house for good.

The following Saturday when Harold came around to pick me up father and mother were getting ready to play a game of cards with our neighbors. Harold told my parents that he was taking me to see another movie and that afterwards we would probably grab a bite to eat like we had before.

The movie he chose was *The Bride of Frankenstein* and I was excited to see a scary film with him. It sounded romantic and I imagined Harold would have to protect me from all the monsters. When Harold drove past the theater I wasn't overly concerned and figured he knew where we were going and trusted his discretion which was my first big mistake.

It was not long before I asked Harold how far out of town the other theater was before he informed me that he had other plans for us that night and said that he had already seen that particular film the Friday before which struck me odd that he had gone alone. Wondering why he'd lied to my parents I asked where we were going instead. Harold laughed and changed the subject saying that he had my mom wrapped around his little finger, which explained nothing. We pulled down long dark driveway where there were a number of cars parked this way and that all over the lawn and I saw there was a large home with a lot of lights on and the music was blaring.

Harold anxiously turned off the engine and announced that we were there. I didn't know where "there," was and questioned him as to what he thought he was doing. He told me to relax and just go with it and said that some friends of his were throwing an impromptu party and that they had invited us to come. When I asked if I knew anyone there he assured me that I would be having a good time whether I knew anyone or not. When I asked what I should tell my folks about where we'd been all night, Harold said that I worried too much and got out of the car. I waited for him to come around and open the door but he started walking up to the house without me and so I jumped out of the car and called out to him to wait for me.

There was no way I was going to walk up to a strange house unescorted, especially when I had come with a date. Harold pulled a bottle of something out of his pocket and offered me a quick drink as we walked along the dark path. I put my hand up and shook my head no and he told me to suite myself and took a quick swig.

"Well if that don't warm you all the way down, nothing will," he said with a shudder and offered me a drink for a second time.

Not wanting to look like a prude I pointed to the bottle and agreed to try it. Coolly I tipped back the bottle and took a big swig like it was nothing at all and it was nothing at all until I swallowed. That big gulp of the revolting liquid burned all the way down and it took my breath away making me cough and shudder wildly while stomping my foot as if that would help the taste.

Harold chuckled at my reaction and took another drink for himself before re-corking his bottle and sticking it back into his pocket for safe keeping. We made our way around a number of vehicles, one of which was moving slightly and had all of its widows steamed up with condensation. Harold saw that I was looking at the car curiously and shrugged it off as though it were nothing for me to worry about but I was worried and asked Harold for another drink; to which he commented that I was a "Good Girl," but at the time I was feeling anything but good and in all honesty I was feeling more naughty than good. My second swig went down a little easier than the first. We stepped up onto the porch and walked inside without knocking. The house was chock-a-block full with people of all ages dancing and drinking and smoking all kinds of things.

"Now this is a party," Harold informed me as though I couldn't recognize where I was.

Harold began introducing me to some of his friends but the music was so loud it was difficult to catch their names. Harold and I made our way through the main room and into the kitchen where there was liquor everywhere and I thought about my father and how he may have liked to have been there more than me. Harold mixed me a drink that tasted much better than the stuff he had on him. The last thing I remembered I was standing in the kitchen talking when everything went fuzzy. I didn't remember going back to his car but evidently I had because the next thing I knew was that Harold's sweaty body was all over me and he was making strange moaning noises in my ear but it was all so vague and disjointed I had hoped that it was all a bad dream but it wasn't.

The thought that this was not the way it was supposed to be, kept running through my mind but I was so drunk I couldn't do anything about it except slap at him and beg for him to stop. What he was doing to me hurt. When he finally stopped it was too late and I found my crumpled bloody undergarments on the floor in the backseat of his car which made me start to cry.

The shock of what had just happened was awful to face and I didn't know what I should do.

Somehow I managed to get out of his car but the ground came up and met me as I threw up in the grass. Fearing I'd gotten what I deserved for drinking I grabbed my neck to check if my mother's pearls were still intact. They were but unfortunately for me I wasn't which sobered me up dramatically and I began hitting Harold and demanding that he take me home immediately. Harold drove erratically while trying to calm me down. He kept insisting that he was sorry and if we weren't drunk it would have never happened. It made me feel terrible that I had allowed myself to get into such a vulnerable place that I couldn't fight off his advances. The whole episode made me feel cheap and sick to my stomach for giving up my virtue like it was nothing. For most of the trip home I starred aimlessly out the window and dreamed I could see a shooting star to wish it all away but no bright spot appeared for me and I knew there was no wishing away what had happened.

All of Harold words rang hollow and insignificant after that night. There was nothing more I wanted to say to him. When he pulled up in front of my house it was late and thankfully, for the two of us, it appeared that my folks had already gone to bed for the house was pitch black and I'd never been so relieved for the darkness in my life. All I wanted to do was to get inside and go to bed where I could bury my head under the covers without being questioned about where I'd been all night.

Harold pulled away while I stood on the porch gathering the courage to go inside. After taking one last deep breath and holding it I quietly turned the doorknob and slipped inside the house and to my room unnoticed. It would have been nice to soak in a hot bath to get the nasty scent of Harold off me but I knew that was out of the question. To protect myself from getting found out I hid my bloody undergarments under the bed until the morning when I took them into the bathroom, locked the door and ran them under the cold faucet until most of the blood stains disappeared down the drain. After wringing them out as best I could I grabbed dry towel and wrapped the wet evidence inside until I could sneak them into the wash without creating suspicion.

Without drawing too much attention I'd stopped volunteering to go to the Amoco station and would have done about anything to avoid seeing Harold but with him working so close to the house there were occasions when I couldn't help catching a glimpse of him every now and then. Mother questioned what went wrong between Harold and me but I refused to talk about it. From that night on Harold avoided me and I avoided him. Nothing came of the backseat incident but when my next menstrual cycle was late I feared the worst. My next period was the only one that I'd ever really looked forward to and rejoiced over when it came.

Nonetheless after the rape I'd lost my way for a time and began seeing a number of other young men, all of whom seemed to want the same thing as Harold. Instead of learning my lesson I started experimenting more with different things and began smoking reefer as well as drinking booze while in mixed company and became a party girl for awhile trying to numb the pain. While under in influence there were a couple of heavy make-out sessions and clumsy fumbling in the backseats of cars. The reefer and booze temporarily eased my guilt but I found as soon as I sobered it all came back to haunt me. Losing my virginity to someone I hardly knew was ugly and created a void in me that I didn't believe would ever go away and there was nothing or no one that could ever make me feel whole again.

One of the boy's I went out with was named, Jim Parker. At first I wasn't overly impressed with him but he appeared to be very attentive and eager to be with me and so I agreed to go out with him. We'd gone out a number of times and it was all innocent until the one afternoon when we went on a picnic and began necking. Our necking turned into heavy petting and the heavy petting turned into having sex. I couldn't call it making love because there was no love involved, just sex and I don't know why I allowed it to happen because I really didn't like it. When Jim reached his climax he pulled out and ejaculated on my leg and as his milky cum ran down my thigh I wondered who I was becoming. There was no reason for me to let it go so far. I enjoyed the necking part of it but felt uneasy about everything else and after that day it seemed Jim had changed his tune too. He became distant and evasive which hurt my feelings and made me want him even more, but by then he did not want me and it was clear.

My next admirer was a young man named Thomas but after Jim I'd already decided that I was going to change the direction and take control back of my life. No more would I let my guard down and do something I didn't want to do. Thomas was a good looking boy and he knew it. His attentiveness towards me shifted suddenly and I began noticing him eyeing up other girls while we were together. It bothered me considerably and made me to feel inadequate and not worthy of his undivided attention.

My feelings of insecurity and shame only intensified when I was with him. His behavior made me suspicious and jealous which were feelings I'd never experienced before. Thomas's wandering eyes bothered me so much I asked my mom what I should do about it and if I should continue seeing him. Her advice was to ignore his bad behavior and that some men were just like that. When she gave me her opinion I felt betrayed and wondered why then she was so hard on dad who as far as I knew never looked on another woman with want in his eyes.

Once, while we were out on a date I thought I would give him a taste of his own medicine and began looking flirtatiously at a certain young man across the room that was also attractive. The minute Thomas caught on to what I was doing he called me out by clicking his fingers in my face and ordering me to look at him and to never mind anyone else in the room.

For me that was the last straw and I told him we were through. There was no need for me to settle and be miserable for the rest of my life just because I had made some mistakes.

Jeff had never made me to feel like Harold or Jim or Thomas had done. He was a gentleman and I wondered where he was but knew that because of some of the things I'd done that even if I found him he wouldn't want me anymore anyhow. Even my father, who might have had his flaws with the drink, wholly loved my mom and no matter what she thought only had eyes for her and her alone. I loved my father and knew that he had more character in his baby finger than Thomas had in his entire womanizing body.

Tensions between me and my mother were palpable as she began to accuse me of turning into a slut. There was one day when mother and some of her friends were playing cards in the kitchen when I walked through and without batting an eye, mother announced to the room, "there goes my whore of a daughter, which infuriated and embarrassed me as I raced to my bedroom and fell on the bed crying in shame.

When the time was right I slipped into the bathroom and slit my wrist with my father's razor but stopped short of going too deep. While sitting on the toilet crying and bleeding Ruby Mae walked in and screamed about what I'd done. It was easily the lowest point in my life and I'll never forget how the first thing out of my mother's mouth when she realized how desperate I'd become was that I was just trying to get attention and that it was a stupid and selfish act and how dare I upset the family like that. It took a few hours but in the end I was glad that my attempt at suicide had failed and promised myself that I would never try the likes again. Life was what you made of it and I was determined that I could turn it around.

Later that same year my mother came into my room while I was sleeping and put my father's shotgun to my head and thought about pulling the trigger. I didn't know anything about it until she confessed her plan to me the next day. Her intention was to kill me, then father and then she herself but she claimed she'd lost her nerve. The way she talked I knew what she was telling me was the truth. When mother confessed that she'd tried shooting me in my sleep a second time I realized the urgency that I needed to move before she found her nerve and went through with it.

CHAPTER TWENTY-FOUR
THE LAST DANCE

Living on my own was tough but I'd managed to put a little money aside and rented a room in a boarding house on the other side of town. Continuing my vocation I found work as a dressmaker at a local shop. The pay was minimal but it was enough for me to get by without any frills. While keeping the room I received the devastating news that my father had passed away. My heart sank as my first thought was that mother had found her nerve and shot him in his sleep but that was not the case. Then I imagined that she might have poisoned him but that was not the case either. The ruling was that father suffered a massive brain aneurism which killed him instantly.

The news of his passing was such a shock it dropped me to my knees. Walking into my Father's funeral was the hardest thing I'd ever done but seeing all the love from his friends helped me in my grief. Dad's death drew a record crowd and chairs were needed to be brought in to handle the overflow at the funeral home. Everyone wanted to be there for him from our old mailman to our butcher and milkman and all the people he'd touched with his wit and humor down at the mill and throughout Pittsburgh and beyond. It was comforting to see so many turn up from all over who genuinely cared and loved him. There were people attending father's funeral that I had not seen in years. All were touched and by father's kind and gentle spirit and reminisced about their favorite stories of something he'd done, said or sang when they were together. Everyone was deeply moved by his passing and even mother was visibly shaken although she never shed a single tear.

Many of the mourners came back to the house where our neighbors brought whatever food they could manage to scrap up and left it for us in father's honor. Mom, Evelyn, James, Ruby Mae and I greeted our guest while trying to console each other in our grief. The loss and emptiness of his absence felt like a cancer eating at my guts and after the last of the attending mourners went home mom asked us to gather father's things and what we didn't want was to be bagged and put out on the porch for donation. Mother had already made the call for the Salvation Army to come by.

Exhausted from the day, Ruby Mae went to bed and I understood, it had been a very long day indeed. For me it was all too soon and I was stunned that we as his children were expected to bag his things up and toss them out right there and then. My father's entire life was reduced to a few bags that were to be set out in the snow. The only thing I kept were a couple of father's monogrammed handkerchiefs, the wooden gun and mount that he and Jeff had put together all those years earlier and one of father's caps that he wore in the winter. After saying my goodbyes I left and went back to my room at the boarding house and fell down on the bed sobbing while wearing father's cap and clutching his handkerchiefs when the door to my room flew open unexpectedly and I got the feeling that it was my father's spirit there to comfort me in my grief.

"Daddy, is that you?" I sniffled getting up from the bed wiping my tears with one of his handkerchiefs.

When I got to my feet I noticed the scent of talc and bracer that father's barber always used after shaving him wafting in the air. My neighbor staying in the adjacent room was winding up his phonograph and had begun playing Guy Lombardo's, "We just couldn't say goodbye," which was one of my dad's favorite songs.

The only thing missing was hearing dad's wonderful voice singing those words, "The clock was striking twelve o'clock, it smiled on us below, with folded hands it seemed to say, we'll miss you if you go," one of the songs refrains. It was like father was there with me and as I wore his cap and clutched his handkerchief we glided around my room in dance until the song was over and his presence left peacefully as if to say he was alright and in time I would be too.

CHAPTER TWENTY-FIVE
HAPPIER DAYS

The decade of woe caused by the Great Depression ended when Japan attacked Pearl Harbor catapulting America into what was up until then Europe's war. The fear of Japan attacking America's Pacific coast on the mainland was thought to be a real possibility. Prejudice against America's Japanese nationals was instantaneous. Notwithstanding the uncertainty of their allegiance all Japanese citizens were rounded up and forced into makeshift concentration camps where they would be held for the duration of the war and it was anybody's guess how long that would be. When America declared war on Japan our James had just turned sixteen. WWII made me reflect on my father's service overseas during the Great War and like mother I hoped the new war would be over long before James was eligible to get involved. I didn't mind sacrificing for the cause but I did not want to lose my brother James.

By the spring of 1942 America was heavily vested and fighting battles all over the world. From Europe to the Pacific brave American lad's was laying down lives and limb for God, Country and Freedom. In order to support our troop effort we on the home front did everything to help contribute. The government instituted a rationing program nationwide. The issued ration stamps were used for our everyday items like clothes, food and fuel for the house and car were rationed, along with everything else we frequently used. A special ration stamp was used to buy the allotted meat, sugar, butter and vegetables we needed to run the house. Other stamps were issued for tires, oil fuel, and gasoline. Posters were plastered on downtown buildings that read, "Do with less so they'll have enough!"

War bonds were purchased and patriotism soared. It was no real hardship to cut back in lieu of what our troops were doing. We busied ourselves by participating in all sorts of drives to collect materials. Commodities such as rubber products were brought in for recycling and scrap metal of every kind was needed and collected in drives. Things from aluminum cans, tinplate, cast iron and any other metal fit for military armaments. We believed in our small effort knowing it could help win the war. Nothing went to waste and everyone did their part ungrudgingly.

From the onset of the war it was clear that America would be an enormous ally for the British and the world. Our factories were quickly converted and began producing tanks, airplanes, warships, rifles and every other war related material needed to do the job overseas. Rosie the riveter came boldly onto the scene and although my name was Rose I was no riveter. My contribution was more related to my experience as a seamstress as I stopped mending and sewing dresses and began working the assembly line stitching seat cushions for Army jeeps.

When James turned eighteen he enlisted in the Navy but before he received his orders the war ended and so thankfully he was spared from being sent to the Pacific to fight. While James was in the Navy Evelyn married a returning soldier that she'd promised to wait for. While mother was cantankerous as ever she took great pleasure in bringing up every mistake and wrong choice that she knew about and warned Ruby Mae not to follow in my footsteps. In spite of mother's influence Ruby Mae was turning into a fine young lady in her own rite.

With everyone going their own way it made me think. So many things had gone wrong in my life and I was tired of having it all thrown up in my face. It was then I had an epiphany and decided I would strike out on my own and make a change. Because city life was all I knew I decided to move north and set my sights on Detroit, Michigan. According to everything I'd heard and read about Detroit it sounded like the perfect place for me and so I bought a train ticket and after rendering my final goodbyes left Pittsburgh for good. It was exciting and I was anxious about my decision.

The train was fantastic and I loved every minute of the ride. Whiling away the afternoon I dreamt of what was in store for me next. While gazing out the train window a great city came into view as the attendant announced that we were pulling into Detroit's Central Station. After a decade of struggles, war, and the loss of my father I was making a much needed fresh start and I felt alive and confident as I disembarked the train. Wandering around the station trying to figure out where I should begin I purchased a copy of the Detroit Free Press and sat down on a bench outside the train station and took note as to who might be hiring within my vocation. My excitement soared when I turned to the want ad section and read an advertisement about a brand new multi floored department store called J.L. Hudson that had just opened and was hiring. By the looks of the ad it sounded very promising.

Walking away from Central Station I felt empowered and happy for the first time in a long time. Because Detroit's streets were set in a grid the directions to the store was simple and I hopped a streetcar and took it to the corner of Woodward Avenue and Grand River. When I arrived the department store was even more magnificent and larger than I imagined it would be. Atop the store was a massive neon red lettered sign that read HUDSON'S and I knew I was in the right spot.

The store was redbrick and had a penthouse that towered high above the street and took up an entire city block. I stood on the sidewalk in awe as I'd never seen anything like it. Even the windows were frosted and emblazoned with an oval etching and the initials, "JLH" in the center of each.

The stores façade at street level was comprised of beautiful polished pink granite adorn with terra-cotta cornices and rosettes. Surrounding the main entrance was ornamental ironwork that complemented the whole shopping experience and I couldn't wait to go inside. My jaw dropped wandering around the first floor and I marveled at the grandeur of their fine jewelry display. Next to it they had watches, leather goods, gloves, belts and a whole array of silk scarf's, hosiery and fashion handbags which were all high end and absolutely gorgeous. As I walked up the stairs I entered the mezzanine where they had a pharmacy, clock shop, watch repair, bookstore, stationery, greeting cards, and the Piccadilly Circus Cafeteria.

The second floor was the men's floor which carried expensive suits, coats, shoes, sporting goods, camera shop and the likes. They even had a post office inside the store. The third floor carried their bedding, bath and to my great relief a sewing center. The fourth floor was devoted to everything children, from infant's layette's, to toddler and teen needs. The fifth and sixth floor was devoted fully to women from its casual dresses and lingerie to formal attire, fine fur's and shoes. After the sixth floor I began taking the elevator up and down. The seventh floor had the millinery hat department, better coats and crystal room.

On the eighth and ninth floor they had interior design in mind with rugs, drapes, curtains and furniture galleries. The tenth floor had china, glassware, silver gallery and fireplace shop. The eleventh floor Lamps, pictures and mirrors. On the thirteenth floor they had pianos, organs, and the music store along with the finer restaurants like the Riverview Room, The Beef Emporium or Pine Room, and the Executive Dining Room.

On the fourteenth floor they had a beauty salon, barber shop and employee cafeteria and I could not wait to apply and could already picture myself working there. The above floors were devoted to marketing and receiving. By then I'd done all the looking around I needed to do and decided to backtrack to the alterations department where I asked the third floor manager for an application. I'd explained that I was new to Detroit and that I had just arrived and was in desperate need of a job.

Reciting some of my accreditations and after a short interview and a referral as to where I could go to find a room to rent Detroit was proving to be an impressive place to live and I loved it from the moment I saw it from the train window. From Detroit's Central Station and wide boulevards too the magnificent J.L. Hudson's where I would now be working, everything was falling into place and I was proud to have been hired by such a company as Hudson's.

The store manager that hired me gave me directions to a nearby apartment that was for rent and so as soon as I left the store I went there to see if it was still available. He said it was clean, cheap and only a few blocks away just off East Lafayette Street and so I walked rather than taking the trolley. Everything was going my way and my new manager's lead worked out as well and I was able to rent the room. Settling into my new surroundings came easy as I unpacked my valise. That evening with everything accomplished that I needed to do I opened my window and sat back and relaxed. It was wonderful to hear a good musician playing a lively saxophone who must have been featured in one of the nearby nightclubs. I thought about going out to find the source of the music but I was exhausted and needed to get some sleep. Not long after I lay down I drifted off to sleep with the cool sound of jazz seeping in through my window. It had been a long prosperous day and for me it seemed that all my dreams were coming true.

Getting up early the next morning left me plenty of time to walk to work. As I strolled along the boulevard I heard some birds chirping away pleasantly in the trees and because I was feeling so satisfied I joined them humming an old song that my father used to sing to me. Everything was clear and bright and right with the world. Eagerly and with purpose I walked through the entrance of Hudson's as their newest employee and took the elevator to the third floor.

My manager, Mr. Dooley kindly met me at the door and upon seeing him I thanked him for the lead on the room informing him that it had worked out fine. Mr. Dooley walked me over to my station and showed me where they kept the fabric and patterns I was to use. In the middle of Mr. Dooley's instructions another girl came rushing into the room and took her seat next to me. As soon as she came in Mr. Dooley glanced up at the clock that hung on the back wall and then back at her with raised his eyebrows as he shook his head. There was no time to make our introductions as she and I began sewing. When our manager left the room she looked over at me and gave a sigh of relief and wiped her brow with the back of her hand and flung her make believe sweat.

"PHEW, that was a close one!"

After the acknowledgement that she was almost late Mary Lou introduced herself to me as I did to her. We chatted some as we sewed and I liked her right away. Mary Lou told me that she hired in about a month earlier and that she really liked her job. She said that Hudson's was a good place to be employed and I had to agree. We were able to take our lunch break together and so the two of us, when the time came left our machines and walked over to the elevator and took it up to the employee's cafeteria where we each ordered the lunch special.

As we sat eating Mary Lou talked about how she'd grown up in Detroit and that she lived near Grand River and Bagley with her folks and by the time it was my turn to tell her something about me, our lunch break was over and we needed to get back to work. After work Mary Lou went her way and I went mine. The next day Mary Lou suggested that for lunch we go across the street to the Sundae shop. She said they had a good menu and the best hot fudge around, I was sold.

The shop she was referring to was called Sanders and Mary Lou was right, everyone in there seemed to be eating the same thing and so that was what we ordered too and it did not disappoint. Sanders specialty was their puff pastry filled with vanilla ice cream and slathered with their famous hot fudge. It was the best dessert I'd ever eaten.

Because Mary Lou had grown up in the area she filled me in on a number of places around that were worth seeing. Running around with Mary Lou was like having my own personal tour guide. For a respite from the bustle of the city, on my days off, I would jump a streetcar and ride it down East Jefferson past the Water Works Park Tower over to Belle Isle.

Like its name, Belle Isle, was a beautiful place that Mary Lou had pointed out to me while showing me Detroit. It was one of my favorite places to go on a warm summer's day and the perfect place for a leisurely stroll around Scott fountain and its four marble lions that guarded the reflecting pond surrounding it. The park had a glass domed conservatory and greenhouse that was filled with every kind of exotic plants and lush flowers imaginable.

From there I'd walk over the humpbacked bridge where lovers canoed and picnicked along the tree lined banks of the stream running through the park. Belle Isle had so much to offer and the view of Detroit along the shore that was magnificent but the one thing I loved most about Belle Isle was its aquarium. The aquarium was comprised with gorgeous blue ceramic tiles and had large thick glassed fish-tanks built into all of its walls. Within the tanks were some of the most odd but wonderful creatures I'd ever seen. Between the tiles and the arched ceiling the aquarium stayed cool, quiet and calm even in the hotter summer months.

After living in Detroit for over seven months I had to admit that my life was good and unbeknownst to me it was about to get even better. While Mary Lou and I were on a lunch break at the Sanders Sundae Shop a handsome man wearing a beautifully tailored suit came walking in. Mary Lou noticed him first and nudged me to look up but I was so busy digging into my dessert I didn't pay much attention to him until he spoke and mentioned Klavon's. His reference caused me to choke into my napkin and wipe the hot fudge off my chin and look up to see who knew about Klavon's and to my dismay it was Jeff. Was I dreaming or seeing some kind of mirage I wasn't sure and for a moment I thought I had to be mistaken but I wasn't. The good looking fellow standing in front of me in the expensive suit was none other than my first love, Jeff Davis from Pittsburgh and I was absolutely gob smacked.

It took me a minute to get my wits about me. I could not for the life of me imagine why Jeff was there and how he had found me. Mary Lou began nudging me harder wanting me to introduce her but I was having trouble finding the words. Jeff came over and asked permission to join us at our table and I would have loved to have had him but our lunch break was over and Mary Lou and I needed to get back to work. As much as I hated to leave I had to go if I wanted to keep my job and I did. As Mary Lou and I walked out of the store Jeff asked where I worked.

"JL Hudson's," I answered pointing in the direction I was going.

"What time do you get off?"

"Six."

"I'll meet you at the door at six fifteen."

Now it had been sixteen years since I'd clapped eyes on Jeff Davis and I could not get over how handsome he'd become. The last time I saw him he and his folks were driving off in that old jalopy headed for Oklahoma and I must have had at least a thousand questions I wanted to ask him and I was sure he had just as many for me.

The wonderful distraction of seeing Jeff again made it difficult to work and I worried I would sew my fingers together. The seam I was trying to sew was just like my mind and all over the place and I had to take it out with my seam ripper and start over. Mary Lou was no help as she kept grilling me about who he was and how I knew him and that I needed to tell her all about the outcome of our meeting that evening. It was all I could do to stay working and I kept looking back at the clock every few minutes.

My day was dragging and the second our shift ended I raced into the lavatory to freshen up before going down to meet Jeff who I knew would be there waiting for me. While looking in the mirror I hated what I was seeing and wished I'd have worn something smarter that day. After sprucing up my hair and pinching my cheeks and biting my lips to give them a little color I found the nearest elevator and asked the attendant named Sam if he wouldn't please take me to ground level. As I felt the floor drop so did my stomach and I knew it would not be long before I saw Jeff.

When the elevator doors sprung open I saw Mary Lou standing nonchalantly over by the handbags pretending to be shopping which made me chuckle knowing what she was up to. I looked over at her shaking my head as she nudged her head and pointed towards the Jewelry counter as if to say he's standing over there. After taking a big deep breath I sucked in my stomach and walked over to where he was. When Jeff saw me he grinned mischievously as if we were about to do something wrong. It was so good to see him and I was really looking forward to spending time with him, so much had happened.

Jeff said that while I was working he'd made arrangements for us to have a window seat at the Riverview Room on the thirteenth floor so I didn't need to go home unless I wanted too. I'd never eaten there before but heard it was very nice so nice in fact the Ford family ate there often. The restaurant was known for its scenic view of downtown and for its Maurice Salad and Canadian Cheese Soup. At first I felt a little uncomfortable about eating dinner in the same building I worked but got over it quickly. Lunch was different. We all used the employee cafeteria most days but this was diner at the Riverview Room. Thinking about spending time with Jeff made any and all anxiety disappear, I knew Jeff accepted me warts and all.

Mary Lou watched from the first floor and rolled her eyes pleasingly as Jeff escorted me back into the elevator and up to the thirteenth floor where we were greeted by the Maitre-d' who escorted us to our table by the window claiming it was the best seat in the house and I dare say that it was. The Riverview Room was very up-scale and I loved it but before the waiter had the chance come over and give us our menus and take our drink order Jeff and I started asking questions simultaneously which made us both of us laugh. Our one burning question was the same.

"What in the world are you doing here?"

We had so much to catch up on and I so looked forward to doing just that. Jeff ordered us a drink and an appetizer. It was so very civilized. We sat there sipping our drinks and talking as though no time had ever passed.

That was when Jeff pulled something out of his wallet and set it in front of me and I practically burst into tears. He still carried that lock of braided hair that I snuck into his valise the day he left Pittsburgh for the last time. When he showed me that I told him about my dad passing and that one of the things I kept was that gun he'd carved all those years ago. Jeff was saddened to hear that my father had died but was deeply moved that I still had that gun. We both laughed when we talked about the day we scared the wits out of my father when he was sleeping on the couch and we stood in front of him holding that gun.

We were jumping from subject to subject when Jeff made the observation that it was more than coincidental that I now worked for J.L. Hudson when my father worked for Jones and Laughlin Steel, J. L. again. I'd never thought of that and was moved to tears when Jeff pointed it out to me again feeling my father's spirit was smiling down upon us. The connection that Jeff and I still had made it seem like all the years of our separation took place in but a wink of an eye and we were both relieved to find out that neither of us had ever married but I felt I needed to confess all. What had happened with Harold and how I went mad for a few months after the rape still haunted me and I wanted to tell Jeff everything but when I confessed that because of the guilt I had attempted to take my own life he stopped me and with tears in his eyes he reached out to me and held my hand.

"Oh Rose, what would I ever do without you," Jeff sighed.

His recognition of the importance of my life made me realize just how thankful I was to be alive and that if I had succeeded back then when I slit my wrist I certainly would not have been sitting there holding hands with the love of my life.

There was no judgment in his voice or heart only love and thankfulness that we had found each other again. It was such a relief for me to confront my demons knowing that Jeff had forgiven all which meant I could finally forgive myself and from that moment on I did.

With confessions made we changed the subject to happier times and began talking about our future together which from that day forward looked bright and promising.

CHAPTER TWENTY-SIX
OUR FAIRYTALE COME TRUE

From the moment I'd stepped off the train at Detroit's Central Station I felt strangely alive and at home. Not only had I succored a dream job and found a place to live close to where I would be working my first day but my long lost love, Jeff Davis, had found me. Yes, Detroit was a special place indeed. It was considered the Paris of the west and like Paris, Detroit was my city of love where magical things happened making all things beautiful. My father had boasted about how beautiful he thought Paris was and I know he would have loved to go back but he never got the chance and never would but oh how I'd wished he could have joined me in Detroit. He would have loved it as much as I did.

Some wishes have no chance of coming true while others can. The wish I'd made upon a shooting star all those years ago had made up for everything. It may have taken sixteen years for it to come to fruition but Jeff Davis was well worth wait. From the moment he'd walked into Sanders Cafeteria and saw me eating a sundae with Mary Lou we were inseparable and our love rekindled.

For us every day was a new adventure. I'd shown Jeff all of the wonderful places I loved visiting in and around Detroit and he continually introduced me to places and things that I might have never discovered on my own. On one of our many excursions Jeff took me out of the country to bordering Canada by ferryboat. The place was called Bob-lo Island, also known as Bois Blanc Island, and it was grand. Jeff planned everything from the picnic we had while there to the afternoon treasure hunt and an evening of dance at Bois Blanc's pavilion.

Although I was a great seamstress, I was not a great cook and so to remedy that Jeff ordered a fabulous picnic lunch from J.L. Hudson's, Mezzanine floor's Piccadilly Circus Cafeteria located on the Farmers Street side. A friend of mine named Minnie worked in the cafeteria and made sure that we had everything we needed for a romantic day out.

Minnie packed our basket with some lovely golden fried chicken, pickled eggs, beet salad and a bottle of white wine. Everything was delicious including her choice of wine. With a perfect meal in tote Jeff and I drove to Bishop Park in Wyandotte where he purchased a pair of boarding passes from the Detroit based Bob-Lo Excursion Co. It was all very exciting and we boarded the Ste. Claire, one of the two huge steamers docked along the Detroit River. The other steamer christened the Columbia had just left by the time we arrived. Both ferries were painted a brilliant white and had multiple levels of open aired viewing. It was such an adventure for the two of us to walk around the decks of the massive ferry that we were on. A loud bellowing whistle blew signaling that our captain and crew were casting off.

Jeff escorted me up a level where we passed a gorgeous stained glass window embossed with an image I'd grown up with. The three feathered crest of the Prince of Wales. Again the Welsh emblem made me to reminisce about my father who was so proud to be Welsh. As we headed over to the viewing deck Jeff set the picnic basket down and we leant on the rail near the front of the boat. As we stood there gazing at the water Jeff kindly pointed out what we were seeing.

Once we were in position and after a couple of short loud blast on the steamers whistle we sailed off peacefully drifting passed Ecorse's Zug Island and into Lake Erie which had rock-lined banks and not much else until Jeff pointed out the lighthouse and the mariner's monument which was a big anchor recovered from the sunken vessel "City of Cleveland." Stands of Birch and Beech trees lined the Island which was why the French called it Bois Blanc. We were told that there were pails of pennies buried all over Bob-lo Island for treasure hunters to find.

That was when I told Jeff that he was all the treasure I ever needed. Upon disembarking the Ste. Clair we made our way to the beach and laid out the blanket and set up our picnic and opened the wine. The setting was idyllic and the company lovely. After eating our perfect lunch we picked some wildflowers and dug for pennies but didn't find any of the buried pails. We gave up on the treasure hunt and Jeff suggested we do something really touristy to remember our time in Canada. It was a wonderful idea and so Jeff and I had our photograph taken standing in a barrel prop with the words boldly painted on the front, "A Barrel of Fun at Bois Blanc Park." It might have been hokey but it was great fun and made for a nice keepsake of our day on Bob-lo Island.

Later that evening Jeff and I danced to the music of Matti Holli and his orchestra at the Albert Kahn Pavilion before reboarding the Ste. Clair for its last trip back to Wyandotte where Jeff had left the car. The Bob-lo boat offered a bit of entertainment and we could hear the band softly playing in the background as Jeff and I took a leisurely stroll around the deck walking hand in hand while enjoying the shimmering moonlight reflecting off the water. Neither of us could believe that we'd found each other again after all those years but were so thankful that we had.

When we landed and left the boat to walk to the car Jeff got down on one knee and pulled out and opened a small box that he had carried with him the entire day. We were in the middle of Bishop Park and if there was anyone else around I didn't know or care because all I saw was Jeff. It was a perfect proposal after a perfect day under the stars on the shore of the Detroit River. Before Jeff could get up or change his mind I jumped into his open arms with a resounding YES, YES, YES, knocking the two of us to the ground laughing!

The very next day Jeff and I went down to Detroit's City Hall and acquired our marriage license and began planning our special day. Everyone was invited including my mother who said she would decline the invitation but surprised me and showed up with our dear Ruby Mae. Both my brother and Evelyn and their families also made the trip north for the event. It was ironic that all those years earlier and unbeknownst to Ruby Mae or anyone else for that matter mother had tried to end her life before it ever began and now Ruby Mae was mother's treasure, caretaker and I don't believe mother could manage without her.

Being the romantic that he was, Jeff had a number of grand ideas about our wedding that I'd never thought of. He was the one that had designed my beautiful engagement ring. The ring had three platinum stars with round diamonds mounted in the center of each star. My wedding band was also designed by Jeff and supported a large emerald cut diamond that had a diamond mounted star on either side. Jeff's attention to detail was nothing less than brilliant. Jeff customized his own cufflinks and tiepin to match my rings and ordered me an accompanying star necklace, earrings and tiara to complete my wedding ensemble. The number of stars used totaled sixteen representing each year we were apart.

Jeff said I could order my own gown from wherever I wanted but I chose to do the measure at the bridal salon at Hudson's. While I was being fitted for my gown Jeff went to Hughes and Hatcher for his suit. Our nuptials were consummated at St. John's Episcopal with Mary Lou standing at my side as my Maid of Honor. Our reception was held at the once wildly popular Hotel Pontchartrain. The Pontchartrain had fallen out of favor with some but we thought it was the perfect venue for us.

The hotel's décor was tastefully refined and designed by Tiffany and Company. Because Jeff had made his fortune in auto design, he always paid particular attention to detail. We both loved the lobby at the Pontchartrain with its scores of soft glistening lights surrounding a series of crystal chandeliers that complemented the Italian black and white marble that led to the front desk and grand staircase with its ornate pillars and hand carved wooden wall panels that were painted pale yellow and had flex of gray and silver running through them.

Our reception was held on the eleventh floor in a banquet room adjacent to its convention hall. Everyone had a wonderful time including my mother and it felt wonderful to be able to share our special day with my family.

Jeff and I had embarked into a fairytale existence and just like in a fairytale I'd found my prince and he his princess. For the pair of us, life was truly grand and the best was yet to come because we were together. Together we shopped around and decided on a house in Detroit's affluent Indian Village. All those years ago Jeff did not have two dimes to rub together and now because of the auto industry and Jeff being so clever we were able to purchased a magnificent home on Detroit's eastside.

Jeff had one more grand surprise to complete the start of our wonderful marriage. Before we left for our honeymoon he had secretly purchased a beautiful collie pup from a breeder. While we were gone he arranged to have the puppy waiting for me. Paris was lovely and we had a grand time but to see our new gorgeous prancing pup was the "creme de la crème," as the Parisian's would say and I of course insisted that we call our new puppy, Star.

A sincere thanks to fellow author Stefan Lorant for *Pittsburgh,* which I found invaluable in my research and a special thanks to my friend Murphy who kindly loaned me his copy of the book.

ABOUT THE AUTHOR
SHARON M. CLARKE

Sharon M. Clarke is a writer and self-taught artist enjoying an enviable life on Anna Maria Island with her husband, Lyn. A part of the baby-boomer generation growing up in the Midwest, Sharon attributes every ounce of her creative prowess to her amazingly clever father, Homer Ping.

Made in the USA
Columbia, SC
20 November 2021

49105784R00129